MILLICENT'S
PRUDENCE

Also by John Snell

My Calf Jack

Doug Times
Eleven Memorable Days that Positively Impacted My Life

MILLICENT'S PRUDENCE

JOHN SNELL

Millicent's Prudence

Windy City Publishers
www.windycitypublishers.com

Printed in the United States of America

ISBN#:
978-1-953294-42-5

Library of Congress Control Number:
2023911623

Cover Photo: Cvandyke/Shutterstock.com

WINDY CITY PUBLISHERS
CHICAGO

Even though this book is fiction,
it is inspired by many stories told to me
by my late great Aunt Millie.
She lived in Germany during
the early days of the Third Reich.
My mother's father, her brother William,
helped her leave before things got out of hand.

This book is dedicated to her.

1

FOLLOW HER DREAMS

Millicent walked slowly with firm steps. She carried her hand made wood cane, painted like the skin of a giraffe, and her large, patchwork pocketbook. She exited through the heavy ornate iron doors of her apartment building near St. James Church on East 72nd Street, New York City, for her Saturday morning trip to Central Park. It was late April. The weather was beautiful. The city was highlighted by bright rays of sunlight between the tall buildings. A light breeze cooled the air. There were no clouds in the sky. It was just after eight a.m.

Millie hoped there wouldn't be anyone sitting on her favorite bench next to the glorious azalea bush near the corner entrance to the park. It would have been quite unusual this early on a Saturday for someone to be sitting there; morning visitors to the magnificent park were usually young joggers. After crossing Fifth Avenue as quickly as she could, as there was minimal traffic, she followed the old curving concrete sidewalk from the park entrance to her favorite bench in the East Green section overlooking the Mall.

As she reached her bench, very tired from her walking, and sat down, she was promptly startled by a flock of geese flying quite low, in formation, directly over her head. She could hear their feathered white wings flapping hard as they forged their way through the cool morning air. She sat down, opened her pocketbook, retrieved her small thermos of fresh coffee she made that morning and removed a square piece of the coffee cake she had made yesterday.

Not only was no one on her bench when she arrived, but this morning there was no one in sight. With few vehicles on Fifth Avenue, near her location it was quiet and peaceful, except for the chirping of morning birds. She looked around after taking a sip of hot coffee to take in the beauty and serenity of the place. She saw it every Saturday, but today she noticed how fresh and green the park was. It was her favorite spot in the whole world. She had been coming here regularly for several years.

A small bird landed on the seat of the bench next to her for a hand out which he received with regularity when she visited her bench. As usual, Millicent broke off a small piece of her coffee cake for the bird, who grabbed it and quickly flew away. By her fourth sip of coffee she had finished the coffee cake completely. She felt very hungry that morning.

Then it happened.

She felt a pain in her right upper arm. She felt some nausea and experienced a great deal of sweating. She was feeling uncomfortable. The pain was growing. She tried to put down the coffee cup on the bench but it fell to the ground. How could this be happening? Not now. She was having a heart attack. In seconds, Millicent was off the bench, on the ground, raising her cane to stabilize herself. However hard she tried, she could not overcome nature. She knew it was the end.

She lay there for about twenty minutes until a jogger saw her lying on the sidewalk in front of her favorite bench with coffee spilled out of the thermos and crumbs of coffee cake strewn about the otherwise clean concrete sidewalk. The little bird came back to see what was happening. The jogger called 911. It was about twenty minutes until EMS arrived to pronounce her deceased and take her away on a gurney. The jogger waited until EMS arrived as a matter of courtesy. He had seen her before on her bench on other days as he ran through the park. In a way he thought he knew her. Little did he know about the life of this heroic woman.

She had been attracted as a young woman to Hitler and the Third Reich in Nazi Germany. She fell prey to the ideology of Hitler. After several years of working for the Third Reich in Germany and being exposed to the horror of the Nazi movement, she went on as a member of the Resistance to help the Allies win the war.

She was born Millicent Bertha Bauer on a freezing day; January 30, 1913, in Gary, Indiana. Her mother, Julia, used to tell the story of her birth. She was born at about 4 a.m. at home with a raging snowstorm outside. Her mother's friend, Ethel, a nurse who lived down the block, came over in the evening and stayed on through the night to deliver Millicent without complications. Her father, William, and older brother, Fred, who was about five years old, watched the whole event. This was not unusual in 1913.

Her early life was good, growing up after World War I. The family had a very nice two-story wood frame house on 508 Bristol Court, a quiet street on which she learned to ride a two-wheeled bicycle with training wheels. Her mother and father provided a good home for her and Fred. Through her early life, in the 1920s, she matured into an intelligent, well-read, pretty and thoughtful young woman.

The 1920s was a time of great success in America. From 1923 until 1928 Calvin Coolidge was President. He advocated for a smaller federal government, lower taxes, less regulation, controlled immigration, limited federal spending, and a strong, healthy, private sector economy. He was non-confrontational by nature making him well-liked by the public.

Many people, Millicent's family included, became quite wealthy while Coolidge was President. People were working, and earned a good wage in a variety of businesses and trades. Her father's construction business, building new homes and renovating existing homes in and around Gary and northwest Indiana, did very well. Her father was a good friend of Roy Owen West who served in the Coolidge cabinet as Secretary of the Interior in 1928 and 1929. Her father built a very nice house for Mr. West in Kenilworth, Illinois. He also obtained some lucrative construction work by having this political connection to Mr. West. Millicent's father's company, Advance Construction Inc., built many service buildings along the newly constructed highways being built by the Federal government in the Chicago area. Times were good. That time in America has become known as the "Roaring Twenties."

But, I am more interested in talking to you about her later life.

It was 1933. Millicent Bauer was 20 years old and living in Chicago, Illinois, with her parents and her brother. After 1929, when the stock market crashed and the depression hit, her parents took some time to consider their options. Should they stay in Gary? Should they move to Chicago? Should they move farther away to California? It was a difficult time for all people. The Bauer's wanted to make an informed well-thought-out decision about staying or moving. After several weeks of consideration her parents decided to move the family from Gary to Chicago in the hope of finding some work in a bigger and more diverse city.

Chicago has always been known as a place to find a job. However, this was during the Great Depression and things were not good anywhere. The construction business thrived in the 1920s before the depression. But in 1933, William Bauer had to close the doors of his company, Advance Construction, Inc., after finishing up one small project at a local doughnut shop, Alvin's Doughnuts, that was expanding into a full-service delicatessen .

Luckily, the Bauers were able to sell the old house in Gary, but they had to take a beating on the selling price. It was purchased by an investor from Indianapolis. With the proceeds from the sale of their house and with some money saved over the years, they were able to buy a small house on the west side of Chicago by taking out a mortgage. It was a much smaller house than their house in Gary, but it had three bedrooms and two bathrooms, which was enough for the Bauers.

In Chicago, William got a job driving a truck delivering bread. His delivery truck was his 1932 Ford pickup which he saved from his construction business. He had to get up at 3 a.m. and make his rounds to hotels, restaurants, and a few private homes before noon. It was an acceptable job but paid very little. One of the benefits was that he could take home any loaves of bread that could not be sold.

Millicent's mother was a seamstress at a local retail store, Goldblatts, which took in old clothes, mended them, and resold them to the public. Millicent did that too. She also helped out at the store at the sales counter. It was not regular work for them, but mother and daughter brought home a few dollars every week. Fred delivered groceries on his bicycle for tips for a local food store, the National Tea.

The Bauer family, except for Millicent, was conservative politically and therefore did not approve of FDR and his phony economic programs. On the other hand, Millicent was a rebel in her younger days, and by the age of 20 she was ready to take on the world. She thought that FDR was making the best of a bad situation, but America was not responding to his social programs.

Of all the things in the world at that time, Millicent was particularly attracted to the societal changes going on in Germany. Her grandparents on both her mother's and father's sides immigrated legally at about the same time to America from Alsace Lorraine in Europe before the First World War. In fact, the families knew each other from the old country. With her German background and from reading press reports in the Chicago papers, she became intrigued about the national socialists and their proposed reformation of Germany. She thought America was struck hard in the gut by the Great Depression and was floundering, even with the government's New Deal programs. She thought that social programs would only make America dependent on the government. She thought that the government was penalizing American business, not promoting it. On the other hand, Germany was on the move.

Her friend Molly who worked with her at Goldblatts told Millicent about her fun at a Nazi youth camp, Hindenburg in Grafton, Wisconsin. She said the kids wore Nazi uniforms and drilled in military style, with marching, inspections, and flag-raising ceremonies. Millicent thought this was the kind of thing she wanted to do. Molly told her that Henry Ford was given an award by Hitler.

What really motivated Millicent was an article by Sigrid Schultz that appeared on February 19, 1933, in the *Chicago Tribune*. The article stated that Hitler promised to save Germany. At a political rally where Hitler spoke in a sports stadium, a huge crowd of about 12,000 people showed up. Hitler promised he would not lie or deceive, he asked the people to go to work, he would develop a future without help from other countries, and Germany would adhere to the eternal laws of history. He promised he would consider the German soil and its people in his governing but not by using theoretical ideas.

At the end of the rally Hitler said, "I implore you, countrymen, to give us four years time to show what we can do. I swear we shall show progress. I swear I am not doing it for money or for pay. I am doing it for your own sake, you my German people."

The event was described in the article as mesmerizing.

Millicent wanted to be a part of this progress to honor her German heritage.

Black, white, and crimson

Millicent wanted to be there.

Her father and mother as well as her older brother, were not pleased with her at all for her interest in Hitler. They believed in the freedom of a republican form of government that America offered, rejected socialism and in the case of the Nazis, fascism. There were many arguments over politics between Millicent and her parents. Many were in German, spoken fluently by the whole family. Many were carried out in loud voices. Many ended in tears. Many times there was silence for days. Most of the time the family members did not talk about their political differences, but such arguments developed mostly at the end of the day, in the evening, when minds were weary and after long hours of hard work.

However, one cold and rainy evening in late March 1932, there was an argument that Millicent would not allow herself to lose. Hitler had become chancellor of Germany in January. He and his supporters were the men with the ideas to transform Germany. It was her time to support this revolution. She could not face another day living at home, during the economic depression, and arguing with her parents. The risks were high but the reward could be wonderful.

And so, the next day she awoke early in the morning in the dark and packed up what little she had into a lockable fabric suitcase with leather straps given to her several years ago by her uncle, William's half-brother Harold. She planned to take a bus to New York City and then a ship to Germany.

Her parents woke up from all of the commotion and were in tears as she packed her bag and prepared to quickly exit the house. Her dad, thinking that she may be leaving for Germany that day, standing before her in his dark blue cotton robe, held her gently by the shoulders and told her he loved her. Then he gave her twenty-five dollars in wadded-up bills with a final departing hug. Her mother, also in her robe, hugged her, kissed her on the forehead, and then collapsed on the living room couch, crying. They loved her. They knew she was no push over. They knew she would survive; she deserved a crack at taking on the world. Fred in his pajamas hugged her as she left the house and kissed her gently on the left cheek.

He said, "If you need anything, anything at all, let me know. I will help you. I love you, Millie."

"I love you too, Freddy."

Her parents watched.

She nodded to him with tears welling up in her eyes. She really loved her brother and would miss him very much. They had survived the good times and the bad times together. The last image she remembered seeing as she walked out of the front door of the Chicago house was the large beautiful multi-colored lamp on the low table in front of the bay window in the living room. The cherubic figures on the lamp seemed to be crying too, although she'd never noticed it before.

Then she walked slowly across the damp concrete porch, in the dim light of a rising sun, and down the front steps to the sidewalk. The curved lower end of the wrought iron railing on the front porch stair caught on her cloth suitcase as if it was telling her not to go. She remembered last fall her dad painting the railing. She kept going. The rail made a slight tear in the fabric on the side of her suitcase.

2

TRAVELING ADVENTURE

Millicent being a thrifty young lady refused to spend any of her money on a cab fare to Union Station in downtown. She walked several blocks to get to North Avenue where several taxis were waiting outside a small local hotel. Even in all of the hustle and bustle of leaving she tried to budget her money well. She had $126 set aside which she had earned working in the dress shop with her mother. She had planned to take a bus from Chicago to New York City and then a ship to Germany. Because she had the $126 set aside, she changed her mind and decided that the train was safer and faster than a bus although it was slightly more expensive. Good thing she also had the $25 her father gave her.

She was the third person in line at the ticket window at a relatively empty Union Station. While she stood in line, she enjoyed the view of the large waiting room at the center of the station. It was massive with an ornate vaulted ceiling and announcements echoing from every corner of the great room. She purchased a ticket in the coach car.

She heard, "Train number six to New York on track #8. All aboard."

She quickly walked to track #8.

When she boarded the New York bound train, there were plenty of open seats in the coach car, so she took over two seats side-by-side next to a window all to herself. It was very cozy. The conductor approved, smiling while taking her ticket. As the great train began to move, she unfolded the twenty-five single dollars from her father and put them in a secret pocket inside the suitcase. She sat on the south side, it being the sunny side of the coach car.

In the side-by-side seats, she had some privacy with curtains in the large window, even though it would be a little uncomfortable sleeping in the fetal position. Most of the scenery along the route was urban. On the south side of the train coach she saw an endless line of empty buildings, some parked cars and trucks, and telephone poles and wires. There was not much else to see since many factories and businesses were closed on account of the Great Depression. At times she would see groups of men, women, and children standing in groups together around steel drums of burning wood to keep warm. What restaurants were open had long lines of men and women waiting for handouts. Seeing the economic hardship conditions along the train route convinced Millicent that going to a rising Germany was better than staying in a fallen America.

In late afternoon, she enjoyed eating a fresh apple that she had bought from a vendor outside Union Station in Chicago before boarding the train. After eating the apple she went to sleep encouraged by the gentle rocking motion of the train. She had an early and full day ahead. While sleeping she missed all of the stops along the way until the train arrived early the next day in Grand Central Station in New York City.

Like she was in a dream, she witnessed the splendor of Grand Central Station in New York City. It was large, loud, and busy. She sat down on one of the long dark wooden benches to take it all in. She had never seen anything like it before. It really was "Grand" and was much bigger than Chicago's Union Station. It had an ornate ceiling similar to Union Station, but much higher. While walking around the station, she got her bearings, exited, and walked west where she knew the boat docks were located on the west side of Manhattan, on the Hudson River. She did not want to waste any time or look like a sightseer.

The weather was cool and clear and she could smell the sea in the light easterly wind. She decided she would walk to the boat docks rather than take a taxi. It was disappointing to see many shops and other buildings boarded up and out of business. She saw many people in line waiting for handouts. Even so it was a grand day for her to focus on her mission. She appreciated the time outside after being cooped up in the train for almost two days. Since all she had eaten in the last two days was an apple, she stopped at a street vendor to buy two hot dogs and a cream soda. She sat on a steel bench with wood slats in front of an attractive stone and brick apartment building to eat. The mixture of the taste of the hot dogs and cream soda with the smell of the sea was very New York.

After several minutes of walking, she arrived at the boat docks, went into the administration building, and asked about any boats leaving for Germany. The man at the counter, wearing a blue cap and jacket and standing behind a steel mesh partition, said he had a ship leaving that day at 6 p.m. What luck! In only about an hour, the SS Leviathan was leaving Pier Number 3 from New York City and was headed for Bremen, Germany, with a stopover in Dover, England. The SS Leviathan was enormous, painted black to just above the water line where there was a red stripe. The railings were white and the smoke stacks were black with a red top ring. She was a very large cruise ship that exemplified her name.

While admiring the large ship, a man came up to Millicent and asked if she was going to Germany. She said yes, but that she did not yet have a ticket. When she explained why she was going to Germany, the man expressed sympathy for the German people and said that the Nazis would greatly improve the country. This older man, named Mr. Ismay, paid her fare, and told her to act like his servant in order to board the ship.

He was a good man, a coal miner by trade. He did not take advantage of Millicent. At the top of the gangplank he slipped the steward a five-dollar bill, in lieu of Millicent's passport. Mr. Ismay's porter carried two large trunks and Millie's suitcase onto the ship. The sloped wood and wire gang plank they were walking on swayed gently as they made their way up to the deck. When aboard, Millicent took her suitcase from the porter, left Mr. Ismay, and went to stay in a small cabin way below deck. She got along well with the crew in the lower deck of the ship. Needless to say she had rather basic accommodations, but they were free and above all, she was on a mission. Her hope to join the revolution in Germany kept her spirits up and burned ever so hot in her young heart.

Travel to Dover was six days. Each day she spent as much time as she could on deck talking to other travelers. She enjoyed standing at the bow with the cool wind hitting her in the face and blowing through her light brown hair. Being on deck several stories high above the water line and feeling the great ship move effortlessly through the cold water was a thrill of a lifetime.

She went to the bow each morning to start her day. Many travelers reinforced her thoughts that Germany was the place to be, not America. Some were interested in joining the German revolution too. Others were on vacation to England. Others were on vacation to Europe.

Mr. Ismay ran into Millicent one day on deck to tell her about his work in Germany including his work in the coal industry. He said his company had been hired to supply coal to the steel mill outside the city of Essen known as the Krupp Steel Works. He explained that Krupp was a major supplier of steel to the Nazis. He also told her he would assist her, if necessary, to leave the ship and enter Germany. She noticed he wore a small gold swastika pin on the lapel of his black over coat which indicated he was connected to or otherwise a supporter of the Nazis. She told him she would appreciate his help, if needed, when leaving the ship.

He politely nodded to her, tipped his hat and went inside the main cabin. Millie stayed on deck in a lounge chair with a blanket until lunch time.

On day six, the final day before stopping in England, Millicent was ever so happy. She watched a few squawking sea gulls hover over the forward deck as the ship plowed through the calm water near the shore. She was happy to see the White Cliffs of Dover. She always wanted to see them. Millicent cried. After the ship docked at the port in Dover, passengers were allowed to get off the ship for one hour. Near the dock she saw many people in line for food, so she left the ship and joined them.

It seemed England had been affected by the depression in America and was having a depression of its own. The food being handed out was fish and chips, common in Britain but new to Millicent, and iced tea. She really enjoyed the free meal. Upon re-boarding the ship and nodding to the Chief Steward standing at the top of the boarding ramp, she made her way to the lower levels of the ship. She noticed a crew change for the trip to Germany. She noticed few passengers getting off in Dover. She did not notice any people boarding the ship in Dover for the trip to Germany.

3

ARRIVAL IN GERMANY

Travel from Dover to Bremen on the Leviathan was two days. The many passengers on deck, including Millicent, formed in a large crowd and moved quickly to the bow to get their first view of Germany. The forward deck of clean teak wood and the busy decorated docks brightened their spirits. Millicent leaned against a railing next to the huge iron anchor attached to the wooden deck with chains and cleats. The wind was blowing in her face and caught her hair. The air was fresh. The sea was a bit choppy, but the great ship proceeded slowly and smoothly. Loud horns were activated with smoke coming out of the smokestacks, as the great ship came nearer to the enormous wooden dock.

As the ship got closer to shore, the crowd saw many black, white, and crimson banners of the National Socialist Party lining the docks, waving in the breeze on both sides of the berth. There was also a Nazi flag being placed on the bow of the ship. The American flag was removed. As this was being done a loud cheer went up from the passengers on deck. Millicent's young heart skipped a beat.

On the near side of the massive dock, German soldiers in small groups lined the edges, grabbing ropes thrown by machines to them which pulled the ship ever closer to the decorated dock. They were getting close enough for disembarking. The large wooden gang planks with rope railings were slowly extended from the ship to the edge of the dock.

What a momentous occasion the arrival was to Millicent. She really felt goose bumps on her arms and legs. This is what she had been waiting for. She wanted so much to join the Nazi movement. She quickly made her way to her room. After packing up her suitcase below deck, she grabbed several sandwiches from the mess hall, placed them in a paper bag for later, and left the ship with the slowly moving crowd of passengers. From the swaying gang plank she noticed Mr. Ismay on the second gang plank away from hers towards the front of the ship. He did not see her.

When she stepped onto German soil, Mr. Ismay came over to her and told her to follow him. It was a good thing she did, because he had to give money, this time German marks, to a Nazi soldier, in a good looking military uniform. He was checking for passports. She smiled at the soldier which may have helped since he let her through the gate and off the wooden plank right behind Mr. Ismay. After arriving in Bremen, on the concrete sidewalk just off the dock, Mr. Ismay told her he would leave her now to go to his house. They hugged very quickly.

Millicent said, "Thank you for everything, Mr. Ismay."

To which he replied, "You are very welcome, my dear. Good luck to you. Heil Hitler!"

Then he and his porter headed for the city with a cart full of trunks. Millicent was very excited and felt inquisitive, so she followed him off the docks toward the city. It was a beautiful spring day in Bremen, so she decided to walk for several blocks and enjoy the scenery. Mr. Ismay turned left after entering the old town area, but she continued to follow the river south of the docks.

The neighborhoods she passed through were very pleasant. Many businesses were open and the streets and buildings were clean and colorful. Buildings had been painted and most had new awnings and signs. In fact, traffic was heavy with many vehicles waiting at traffic lights at intersections. She got out the sandwiches from the ship and ate while she walked along. After walking for many blocks in the old town area, she stopped at a park bench to finish eating. While she ate, she noticed a new storefront with colorful Nazi flags and banners out front and several uniformed soldiers smoking outside the front door. They stopped her to ask if she needed directions. She mentioned her interest in joining the Nazi party.

They immediately asked her to enter the politically decorated building which appeared to be a recruiting office. After a half hour of questioning by a Nazi soldier, during which she spoke German, and then having her picture taken, she was accepted as a worker in the Nazi Party. They gave her an identification card with her picture on it. The card gave her address at a work camp in the City of Dachau. She would be working in the soldier's kitchen at the prison camp in Dachau. She was excited to have a job. The soldier explained they were trying to fill these much-needed positions. He also explained she would be happy working there. After taking an oath, she was given $100 German marks and a free stay, including meals, at the Turmhotel Weserblick nearby.

The hotel was just down the street, so with instructions from the Nazi soldiers outside, she walked to the hotel carrying her suitcase in her left hand and her newly issued Nazi uniform on a metal coat hanger over her right arm. She could not believe it. She felt her eyes water. She was happy. The air temperature was dropping slightly as the sun was setting which created long red and orange shadows along the narrow streets. After checking in at the hotel and taking the elevator to room 202, she fell onto the bed and quickly fell off to sleep. She did not wake up until the following morning. She really needed to sleep, especially in a nice bed. She dreamed of her parents and Freddy.

Millicent was sleeping soundly in the early morning when she was interrupted by a loud knock on her door. It was a pleasant morning. The clock on the nightstand showed 6:05 a.m. She put on a red robe furnished by the hotel and looked through the peep hole in the door at a handsome young man in military uniform, shifting from foot to foot.

"One moment," she said. She ran into the bathroom, brushed her hair quickly, returned to the door and partially opened it.

A tall soldier with blond hair and blue eyes was smiling as he said in English, "Good morning. I am Lyman Hoffer.

I am here to take you to your assigned job." His German accent was very cute.

She thought quickly and told him, "Please, go to the lobby and wait for me there."

"Miss Bauer. I will wait outside your door."

"Very well, Lyman Hoffer."

After examining again, this time in detail, the uniform given to her at the recruitment building, she folded it neatly and packed it in her bag. It was a black and white uniform. The kind a restaurant worker would wear. Thank goodness it was not a soldier's uniform. She took a quick shower and got dressed in a skirt, blouse, and sweater she brought from home. Everything else she packed in her suitcase, except she put on walking shoes issued to her. They turned out to be quite comfortable. She assumed they would not be coming back to the hotel. She made a quick look around the room to see if she had left anything behind and quickly opened the ornately carved heavy wooden door to see Lyman standing there.

He said, "Good morning, Miss Bauer. You look very nice."

"Thank you, Lyman Hoffer."

"Please call me Lyman."

"Okay, Lyman," she said with a smile.

Lyman and Millicent then walked together down the carpeted corridor and got on the elevator. While they waited, Millicent noticed how beautifully decorated the hotel corridor was. The ceiling was trimmed with wood crown molding, the walls were plastered with a rough finish and the oriental carpet was trimmed by a very high wood base. The lighting was from candelabra-style lights and metal wall sconces. There was a rich visual feel to the hotel.

When the elevator arrived, the operator greeted them and promptly took them down to the lobby. They had a nice breakfast at the small restaurant adjacent to the lobby of the quaint hotel. Everything seemed to be in order and friendly in a business sort of way. Millicent had very good pancakes and a cup of dark brewed coffee. Lyman had scrambled eggs and a coffee. He paid cash to the waiter. He had a car waiting at the curb in front of the hotel.

It was a small black four-door Mercedes. It looked like an official military vehicle. The driver, dressed in a dark suit with black tie and white shirt, took them quickly to the local train station at Bremerhaven only a few miles away. Out in front of the train station were many other recruits with their military escorts waiting along with other uniformed soldiers. When notified over the loudspeaker system, they all walked through the well-kept, beautiful but small train station and boarded the train.

Lyman helped Millicent with her heavy bag and placed it in the overhead rack above their seats in coach. It was not more than 20 minutes before the steam locomotive and its following train pulled slowly out of the station. The train ride, with its comfortable seating and Lyman as company, did not seem that long to Millicent.

The other recruits and their escorts were engaged in loud conversations. The passenger car was alive with talking. Lyman told Millicent she would be working in the kitchen for soldiers at a work camp in Dachau near Munich. He said there were several other recruits on the train going to work at the same camp. He assured her that work would be easy and she would be paid well starting at 74 marks per week. She would have time off each week for recreation. She would work four days, eight hours a day, and be off three days each week.

They discovered they had a love of railroad trains in common and were exactly the same age. The train was half passenger cars and half freight cars, pulled by a DR Prussian P-10, 2-8-2 steam locomotive with huge red driver wheels. This type was referred to as a "Mikado." The sound of the chugging of the locomotive, and the smoke coming out of the stack as well as the steam was familiar to both of them. They became fast friends. The scenery of the woods of Germany with the strong sunlight pouring through flew by them as they talked. At the end of the journey, the train pulled into a station that was located at the Dachau work camp. Millicent thought this was odd. Lyman explained that trains were used for passengers and material supply for the ongoing construction.

As the train slowed down, blowing its whistle, and ringing its bell, the work camp could be seen. It was a very large development and was very intimidating with its barbed wire fence having a curved top portion of razor wire and four very high guard towers with armed soldiers in them. After the train blew its whistle again and stopped, Millicent and Lyman stepped off the train into the work camp train station. The massive concrete platform with newly painted steel pipe handrails had a stair and a ramp with a stone pathway that led to the heavily fenced area of the camp. The recruits and escorts were guided down the concrete sidewalk to a large fence and gate that protected the buildings outside the work camp yard.

A large military truck carrying a dozen or so Nazi soldiers rushed past them as they were standing on the concrete sidewalk outside the gate. Millicent was startled. She looked up at Lyman's face with a smile. It was a nervous smile. He smiled back and very gently put his hand on her lower back to comfort her.

4

THE PRISON CAMP: DACHAU

As Millicent suspected from the appearance of her issued uniform, she was assigned to work in the soldier's kitchen at Dachau. This prison camp had just recently opened, in a beautiful location just south of Munich. It was exciting to Millie in every way. Construction was going on in several locations in the camp inside and outside the fence. There were many prisoners in striped uniforms working on the construction projects. Many guards in uniform were supervising the construction work.

All of the buildings she could see as she and Lyman walked through the gate towards the kitchen dining facility were brand new. The buildings were simple in design, clean, and had a natural style of light stucco and dark wood trim around square windows and doors. Each building had steep sloping dark wood shingle roofs. Outside the high barbed double wire fence, the kitchen stood out as a separate building from the administration building, the motor pool building, and the staff barracks buildings. Apart from the administration, kitchen, and staff barracks buildings inside the high wire double fence stood many stark unpainted and crudely constructed wood barracks for the prisoners. Millicent was to help with feeding the military guards and staff. Others were responsible for feeding the prisoners.

Lyman took Millicent to the administration building on the way to the kitchen building so he could check in and introduce her to the camp director, Col. Wackerle. Lyman asked her to wait in the lobby of the administration building while he met quickly with another soldier before entering the Colonel's office. The lobby was a large carpeted square room in the corner of the administration building. Jane, the receptionist, about Millicent's age, a stunning brunette with brown eyes, smiled and politely nodded to Millicent. Millicent smiled and nodded back to her while she waited in the lobby.

In what seemed like a minute, Lyman left Millicent's suitcase in the lobby and escorted her into the large corner office. The room smelled like it had just been painted, and the windows were clean and clear as if they had just been installed. Original works of art were displayed on each wall. A photo of Hitler hung behind a large mahogany desk. From this office there was a spectacular view of the garden and the neatly kept grounds facing outside the camp toward the beautiful wooded hills nearby. Col. Wackerle, a short bald man with a scar on his left cheek under his eye, stood up to reach over his large desk and shook Millicent's hand. He asked if she spoke German. She nodded yes and indicated she would be pleased to assist with translations from English if needed.

He thanked her and said in German, "Millie, work hard and have a good attitude."

She said, "Ya, mein Kommandant."

They all laughed.

The Kommandant and Lyman gave each other the heil salute. Millicent also gave the salute following their lead. It was her first of many. The Kommandant then shook her hand again and Lyman and Millicent left the office. Millicent's heart skipped a beat as she grabbed her suitcase and left the building with Lyman. They both nodded and smiled at Jane on their way out. Jane smiled and nodded back.

Next they walked past the kitchen to the female barracks so Millie could settle in. It was late afternoon and some kitchen and other types of workers were returning to the barracks after putting in a long shift. The female barracks leader who also worked in the kitchen was already in her private room at the far end of the barracks. She was the only one with a private room. Lyman pointed her out and told Millicent her name was Frieda Miller.

He said, "Frieda is a good person."

She wore the outfit of a kitchen worker, the same one everyone working in the kitchen wore. The uniform consisted of a white cloth head covering, a black dress with some white accents, a large white apron, and black stockings with black leather low heel shoes. Everyone was also issued a jacket and slacks, several T-shirts and shorts, an informal dress, and three gray cotton blouses.

Frieda, a short, thin woman in her mid-fifties, with brown hair in a bun, was on her knees busy looking for something in her footlocker when over her shoulder she first saw Millicent and Lyman. Frieda's very neat room had a bed, a desk with a telephone, the footlocker and a standing armoire. She immediately rose to her feet, smiled and approached both of them with enthusiasm. However, she was very businesslike. It was not often an SS guard was in the women's barracks.

She said to Millicent in German, "Welcome to Dachau. I heard earlier you were on your way. What a neat, clean person you are. You shall fit in nicely. When most of the staff returns here in a short while I will introduce you. Please stand by." Millicent was impressed by her professional attitude. She smiled and felt that she would be happy to be working for Frieda. She also understood from Lyman that Frieda was a strong woman and not to be trifled with.

Millicent responded in German, "I will be most happy to work hard for you, Frau Miller."

As more women workers entered the female barracks, the noise level rose, and Lyman excused himself. He told Millicent he would catch up with her later. She waved at him as he left. A big strong man he was. Millicent caught a view of him through a window near Frieda's room walking quickly down the sidewalk to the administrative building. After Lyman was out of site, she became a bit nervous about waiting outside Frieda's room. The female barracks consisted of a large room with wooden over/under bunks. At one end there were two private rooms, one of which was Frieda's, and at the other end there was a toilet room with gang showers and a utility room.

Millicent was a little uncomfortable standing in the partially occupied bunk room until Frieda said, "Not to worry."

And she didn't.

Millicent found a spot on a lower bunk around the corner from Frieda's private room that had its bedding unmade but had sheets, pillowcases, towels, and a mattress carefully placed on the metal spring support. Frieda nodded her head at Millicent to indicate that bunk was good for her. Millicent waved back and smiled. After several minutes Millicent made her bed, unpacked and tried on her work uniform.

Frieda called the women together in a small open space outside her office. There were forty-two women present in uniform, two in civilian clothes, and two in their robes assembled when Frieda said, "Girls, we have a new member of the team, Millicent Bauer. She will work the third shift and report to Renee. Let's all welcome her with a spritely round of applause. Thank you."

Happy faces and generous applause filled the room which made Millicent smile and her eyes water a little. She felt that this was the right thing to do. She then looked for Renee, who was already coming over to her to welcome her. Renee was in charge of the midnight to eight shift called the "graveyard shift."

Renee, a flaxen-haired, blue-eyed, tall, well-built girl, was grinning and bubbling over when she approached Millicent and blurted out, "Welcome, welcome, welcome. You will not be disappointed. We will start tonight at midnight and work through breakfast and be off duty at eight in the morning. Then sleep. Mostly clean up from the second shift and then the hungry breakfast crowd. Come, I will take you over to the staff dining hall and kitchen to show you the lay of the land."

Millicent was impressed at Renee's friendliness and her energy. She thought they were about the same age.

"I will work hard and you will not be disappointed," said Millicent.

Frieda nodded approval to Renee and suggested that they see if there was anything left over to eat and drink. The two girls looked at each other and felt an immediate bond between them as they left the barracks.

The staff dining hall was next to the women's barracks for good reason. All the workers in the dining hall and kitchen were women. The two arrived in several minutes running into Marsha just inside the main entrance door. She waved at them. Then touching Renee gently on the shoulder, as she breezed by them, she exited the building to join the others in the barracks after her shift. Marsha was a heavyset younger girl with long sandy colored hair. The second shift had just started and the first shift was leaving the building. When Millicent and Renee went into the kitchen there were several good looking ham and cheese sandwiches made up but not eaten in the cooler. There was plenty of juice left too.

Before too long the girls were talking about their lives, their loves, and their hopes, as the sandwiches and juice slowly disappeared. As they were talking, they both realized they had joined the Nazi movement for the same reasons. To be part of the movement to benefit the German people. This was a bond Millicent was looking for. At about nine o'clock, Renee suggested they get a little sleep before starting the midnight shift. Both girls were happy in their souls to have met one another.

When her clock alarm sounded at eleven-thirty sharp, Millicent was up, out of the shower, and getting dressed when Renee came over to walk with her to the kitchen.

"Good morning, recruit."

"I am ready to go. Please call me Millie."

"Okay, Millie."

Then Renee giggled.

Millie's first assignment from Renee was to make sure the coffee pots were clean, and coffee was started. This entailed using a strong cleaning solution in the coffee urn and thorough rinsing as well as washing the internal percolation parts. When she had cleaned the coffee urn, she set it up, adding coffee grounds and water, and turning it on to percolate. Following directions, she added a teaspoon of salt into the coffee grounds to cut the bitterness. The four coffee pots were ready and full of coffee in about fifteen minutes. She was able to find another ham sandwich left over to have with her coffee for breakfast. She felt good that she was able to help. The experience helped her to feel part of the team.

The early morning went by quickly. The breakfast rush was average according to Renee. Millie kept the coffee coming. She also assisted with waiting on tables to clean them off so new arrivals had a clean place to eat. She learned how to swap out an empty milk container for a new one in the milk dispenser. The full containers were very large and heavy which required all her strength and agility to replace them.

After the breakfast crowd was gone, the sun was rising and the girls on the "graveyard" shift sighed a bit of relief. Clean up of the building as well as the kitchen itself was a priority. Millie and another girl, Jean, were responsible for mopping the floor due to the size of the building. Millie took the dining area and Jean took the kitchen itself. Millie had a larger area to mop but the other girl had a dirtier floor to mop. She showed Millie how to clean out the bucket and mop and how to store them properly for reuse. Millie was thankful for Jean's unsolicited help. When they were finished they walked together back to the barracks. They both took a much needed shower with the other "graveyard" shift girls and went to bed. The sun was shining brightly and birds were chirping as Millie finally closed her eyes and fell off to dreamland.

The last thing she heard before falling asleep was a train carrying freight cars full of people entering the work camp station.

5

A RIDING VACATION

It took Millie three days to get into the swing of it but after three weeks she was identified as one of the best new workers at the dining hall. After three months, she was Renee's right-hand girl. Many happy, hard working months passed by before Jane, in administration, suggested going away for an upcoming three days off. She suggested this to only Millie, Renee, and Marsha.

Jane, who was a friend of Renee's, both having grown up in Berlin, knew about a hotel named the Hotel Geiger, relatively close by the camp that was affiliated with a riding stable. She suggested to the other girls they could go horseback riding and stay at the hotel. The four girls thought that was a fantastic idea, would be lots of fun and also, a great way to see the local German countryside, including cute German men. Jane had access to a car in the camp motor pool used by the SS trainees, like Lyman, who were stationed at the camp. These vehicles were used to go outside the camp on military duty and also for personal use.

The next three days off was in ten days, so Jane had to operate quickly to get the plan executed. It was not long before Jane had gotten Col. Wackerle's approval for the car and the outing, made a reservation at the Hotel Geiger for two rooms, and made reservations for four horses at the Wittenberg Stable. She also cleared the recreational activity of the kitchen workers with Frieda. Things seemed to be shaping up well for the girls' vacation.

The day of the start of the vacation rolled around very slowly for the girls. On the day before they were to leave, Renee, Marsha, and Mille were so energized and happy that Frieda actually smiled at them as they left the dining hall on Friday, their last day before leaving.

Each girl had already packed a bag for the trip. Millie packed her uncle's old suitcase with changes of clothes and toiletries, with room left over since the bag was so large. As she packed it that Wednesday evening, she remembered her awful departure from her parents and Freddy. The corner of her suitcase was ripped she remembered on the steel handrail at the base of the front steps. However, her life was now hers and she was making the best of it in Germany. In fact, she was proud of herself. She had a good reputation and friends with whom she was going on vacation. She was thankful for having trustworthy friends. Tomorrow would be the start of a good vacation that she would long remember.

Saturday morning was a glorious day in late June. The hills around the camp were highlighted by the early morning sun as Jane pulled the car, a small BMW coupe, around to the front of their barracks. Jane opened the trunk to inspect the spare tire and jack just in case of an emergency. All was in good shape. The girls, dressed in civilian clothes, brought out their suitcases and bags and packed them in the tiny trunk. When outside the camp, they had to look good to the public. The BMW was barely big enough for all of the gear they were taking, but everything fit after some adjustment. It was seven in the morning before Jane drove out of the main gate and they waved at the guards. The drive was about two hours, short and happy. It did not seem long before they arrived at the Hotel Geiger.

The hotel, nestled into the woods in a valley between two high mountains, was a series of buildings, the largest of which was three stories high with a separate wing off to the side. In front was an extensive beer garden with strings of lights and a spacious veranda over the main entrance doors. Lots of vegetation around the hotel made it warm and inviting. The design was typical German white stucco with dark wood trim and a wood shake steep sloped roof. The lobby was not extravagant like the hotel in Bremen. In fact, the entire hotel was country style with hardwood floors and exposed beam ceilings throughout including the bedrooms.

Their check-in was easy. The hotel had a laid-back atmosphere. Mr. Geiger, the owner of the hotel, was seated behind the front counter when they arrived. He was a short man with sleek combed back hair dressed in a dark suit, white shirt, and red tie. He was friendly to the girls, getting up and coming around the counter, and gently hugging each one.

"Welcome to the Hotel Geiger, the oldest and finest hotel in southern Germany. If I can be of help you in any way, please let me know," he said in German.

"Thank you, sir," said Jane.

He responded, "Your two rooms, 302 and 304, are on the third floor. They are very nice, with balconies."

As the girls got on the elevator, there did not appear to be any people in the lobby and only a few in the restaurant. The elevator operator, who was named Fred, took them to the third floor and gave them directions to their rooms. Jane gave him a tip. Even though there were few customers in the hotel, there were four military guards between the lobby and the parking lot. Germany was an authoritarian military state. Each guard was armed.

The girls had decided on the drive that Millie and Renee would stay in one room and Jane and Marsha would stay in the other. Their rooms were adjoining with their balcony facing the front of the hotel overlooking the front beer garden. Even though it was an old hotel, it was clean, and the beds were comfortable, not like the atmosphere at camp. After choosing which bed they wanted, Mille and Renee opened the door between the rooms and looked over Jane's and Marsha's room. It was the mirror image of their room.

"Pretty fancy room isn't it, Jane?" asked Millie.

"You bet," responded Jane.

"Let's get lunch, guys," said Marsha.

"Follow me," said Renee.

Back in the lobby, the girls picked up a brochure on the Wittenberg Riding Stable which was just down the road. From the brochure they learned the stable was open that day and the trails went through the wooded countryside around the hotel.

They were seated in the restaurant which was just off the lobby. Their table was near the center of the dining area. The dining area was simply decorated with several animal heads mounted on the walls. There were only another couple of tables occupied for lunch. Each girl ordered a garden salad and a chicken sandwich. Lunch was served promptly and enjoyed by all. What a pleasure to be waited on rather than waiting on someone else. An accordion played quietly outside in the beer garden. They all were in high spirits and in vacation mode.

After lunch, the girls drove to the stables just five minutes away. Because Jane had called already, as recommended in the brochure, Mr. Wittenberg had four horses waiting out front for them. Each girl paid her own bill. They were to take the "red" trail. Mr. Wittenberg told them to put on riding boots he had in the stable. Then he outlined some rules. The first rule was to be kind to your horse. Then he showed them how to mount and dismount properly. Also, he showed them how to cue a horse for walking, turning, and stopping. After he demonstrated each command, each girl practiced on her own horse in a small corral just outside the barn.

Millie's horse was named Ruth. Jane's was named Baby. Marsha's was named Attica, and Renee's was named Biggy. Ruth and Biggy were both beautiful Chestnut in color and Baby and Attica were both Bays.

The red trail was easy to navigate, was mostly flat, but had fine views of the surrounding hills. The winding dirt trail, flanked with underbrush and small tree growth, was marked by red blazes on trees and posts along its route. According to the brochure, the red trail was two hours. That is if the girls did not get lost, which they did not.

There was a lot of quiet time at the start learning the ropes of horseback riding; but after a few minutes, once the giggles started, it was all over. Baby and Attica had to poop on the trail, which got everybody excited; but the ride went so well, they planned another for the next day. As the horses walked along the trail, Millie thought how beautiful this part of Germany was with the sun shining through the dense forest around them. It reminded her of when her family visited Wisconsin to see the Dells. The topography and deciduous tree growth were very similar, she thought.

As if a song was playing in her head, her horse Ruth, who was directly behind Jane on her horse Baby, swayed to one side and then the other as if she had done this many times before. She had. In fact, the horses followed each other on these trails almost every day. After a stunning two-hour ride on the trail through the woods, as they returned to the stables, and after they dismounted their horses, each girl rubbed the face of her horse to say thank you and goodbye. Millie fell in love with her horse Ruth. The other girls fell in love with their horses too. What a fine day.

Back at the hotel the girls went up to their rooms and had quiet time before dinner. Millie read a brochure from the hotel on care of horses. Jane played her radio, and Marsha sat on the balcony admiring the beautiful scenery. Renee sat outside on the balcony of Millie's and her room and talked with Marsha across the guardrail.

The sun was turning dark red and gently setting into the forested hills to the west when Jane said, "Let's go down to the dining room."

Without hesitation the girls left their rooms, met in the hallway, and took the elevator down to the lobby. Fred was still on duty.

Fred asked, "How did you like horseback riding?"

Each girl complemented the Wittenberg Stables and explained how much fun they had. Jane mentioned they wanted to go out tomorrow on the "blue" trail but could not because they had to get back to Dachau.

"Very good, very good; however, that trail is tougher," said Fred.

Jane responded, "Yes. However, we must go."

An accordion playing with a violin could be heard above the noise of the many patrons eating and talking in the dining room. Dinner was a buffet style, so the girls could sample the food as they desired. Millie and Jane stayed with German food, while Renee and Marsha went for Italian. Rolls which were made fresh every day in the hotel were served with dinner. They were brought by a waitress to the table in a small wicker basket with cloth over them, still warm from the oven. With butter and strawberry jam, they were simply delicious.

Dessert of apple strudel and coffee was included as part of the buffet. The meal was a happy time for them. Again they were thankful they were the served not the servers. After thanking Mr. Geiger for the wonderful buffet, they took the elevator to the third floor and retired to their rooms. They had a full day of adventure. They would sleep well that night.

The four armed guards, who the girls thought were very handsome, walked the hallways of the hotel all night.

SS Leviathan

Guards at the Gate

Kitchen

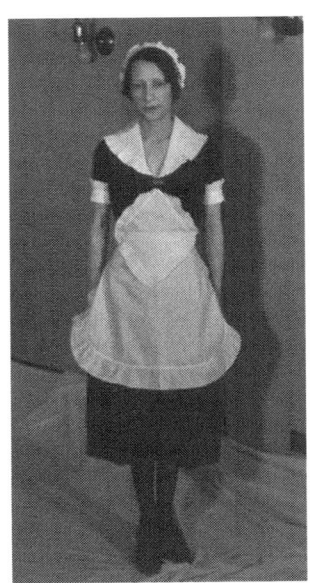

Kitchen Uniform

Horseback Riding

Beach Fun

Hotel Geiger

Enigma Machine

6

BEACH VACATION

It was 1938. After working in the kitchen for several years, Millie was assigned special duty to be in charge of training the new kitchen staff. Ten women had left the previous year for greener pastures leaving the hard kitchen work to those left behind. Frieda thought Millie would be good trainer for the replacement staff. She was right. Millie worked out perfectly. The ten positions were filled right away and each person hired worked out fine after their training.

On a particularly difficult workday, at noon, in heavy rain, lightning, and thunder, ten prisoners were hanged in the front courtyard. Millie was upset about the hangings, particularly on that day, but rationalized it was just a part of prisoner control. The next day, Jane asked Millie if she would like to get away from it all and to go to a beach. It was getting to be the end of summer but weather conditions were still favorable for swimming in the Mediterranean Sea. Jane had already asked Renee and Marsha. Not surprisingly, they both wanted to go. Of course Millie wanted to go too.

With the Commandant's and Frieda's approval, and as a reward for their hard work and loyalty, they took off Friday through Monday. They would have fun on the beach for two days and drive the other two days.

Jane made the arrangements for the car and hotel. This time, the car was a large black Mercedes sedan with leather seats and much more interior room and a larger trunk than the car they took to the Hotel Geiger. The trip to their destination, Genoa, Italy, and the Camogli Beach, Liguria, one of the finest beaches in Europe, was about an eight-hour drive. There was a good place to stop about halfway in Ville Franche-Sue-Mer. Jane had been on a beach outing some time ago with her husband John and knew the way, where to eat for lunch, where to stop for gas, and where to stay in Genoa. The four girls were very excited as the Friday of their departure approached.

There was an increase in the number of guards assigned to Dachau. The camp's population of prisoners was increasing as the Third Reich invaded Austria. Also, Dachau was being used by the military as a training camp for the SS as well as a prison camp. The camp had a new Commandant, Theodor Eicke, who released new regulations governing the camp's operation. Prisoners who did not follow the new regulations were executed. With more guards to feed, work at the camp was becoming very hectic for the girls in the kitchen. At the last weekly staff meeting, Frieda explained how Germany was ridding the countries it was bringing into the Third Reich of their political prisoners, socialists, and communists. There were also prisoners of war at Dachau. Frieda explained to the women, particularly at this time, not to approach the fence around the prisoner area or talk with any prisoners. She explained that they were dangerous.

After the staff meeting, Millie stayed behind.

She asked Frieda, "What is going on here at the camp. I am very worried."

Frieda said, "It has been reported that families are being imprisoned here who are not war combatants because they are Jewish. I am disturbed about this. I think that the government is confronted with a problem of taking over some countries but does not know what to do with the Jews, except kill them."

Millie thought her original feelings for Hitler and Nazism, and the reason she joined the movement to help the German people may have been wrong. How would she handle this?

When Friday at 7 a.m. rolled around, Jane filled up the Mercedes with fuel, the girls packed their bags, loaded a previously made-up picnic basket of snacks and drinks, and they were off. They were at ease as the guards at the gate cleared them to pass through. They were looking forward to being outside the camp. As the camp disappeared in the rearview mirror, each girl shared a sigh of relief. Millie worried about what Frieda had told her. She also worried about the new girls she had trained being able to perform, and whether Frieda would be pleased with her training efforts. But the girls were in the wind and were already enjoying a long weekend.

Jane drove the first leg and Marsha the second. They both were pleased with the performance of the car. It was powerful, big, roomy, and very comfortable inside. John, Jane's husband, and the chief of the motor pool staff had washed the exterior and thoroughly cleaned the inside of the car the previous day.

Riding in the vehicle with its powerful, yet quiet engine through the winding mountain roads was practically a pleasure. At all check points and national borders they were waved through without stopping since the car was flying Nazi flags on both front fenders. They did not have to pay any tolls either. They got through the Gotthard Tunnel without any problems.

Then, about midway, they stopped as planned by Jane, at the La Mere Germaine restaurant in Ville Franche-Sue-Mer. It was touted to be a great restaurant and it was. It was also worth the money. They ate a fine lunch of wiener schnitzel and spaetzle with a glass of sparkling water on the large wooden deck outside the restaurant overlooking the Alps. Wiener schnitzel is a cutlet of veal pounded thin by a meat tenderizer, then dipped in flour, egg, and breadcrumbs and fried until golden. Spaetzle or German pasta comes from the word *Spatz*, which means "little sparrows." As they all sat there, a fresh cool wind blew up though the girls hair, blowing Jane's napkin away. It was quickly replaced by the waitress. Millie used her napkin to dry her eyes. She cried to herself. She was with good friends, away from work, and on a long overdue vacation.

Millie drove the leg after Renee. For safety Millie turned on the car's headlights. It was not as difficult a drive as Renee's drive through the Alps. They entered Genoa late in the afternoon. Jane gave directions to guide Millie to the hotel, Palazzo Grillo, located deep in the oldest part of the city. Millie carefully pulled the car up to the main entrance. The car was parked by a valet and their bags were handled by the concierge. This allowed the girls to check in right away at the front desk. Millie tipped the valet and Jane tipped the concierge.

The hotel on the exterior was vintage 1545 and was recently converted into a first-class modern establishment. The building structure itself was a magnificent example of 16th century architecture. Millie was particularly impressed by the ornate original exterior and the preserved interior portions of the hotel. She remembered that the 16th century in Italy became known as the *Renaissance*, which means *born anew* in French. Millie imagined her life now as "born a new." Still, she thought about her parents and Fred and prayed they were safe, as she and the girls made their way to their rooms.

Their rooms were on the second floor overlooking the beautiful piazza in front. In their rooms, because of the long drive, they were more tired than hungry. They ate some of the snacks that were left over from the trip, took showers, and went to bed. Jane and Millie shared a room and Renee and Marsha shared the adjoining room. They agreed to meet for breakfast at 8 a.m. in the lobby. Millie and Jane talked for an hour or so before falling fast asleep. They agreed that their lives had tuned out better than they expected. Millie prayed that her decision to serve in the Third Reich was the right one.

The next day, they ate a continental breakfast in the dining room before taking a shuttle to the celebrated beach in Camogli, a beautiful local beach near the city. The weather was perfect, warm but not too warm, with a slight breeze off the water. The smell of the sea was unusual and very pleasing. Each of the girls wore a light blouse and loose slacks over her swim suit, and each carried a towel. Marsha carried the picnic basket which had a few snacks left over. Even so, they bought snacks and drinks at the concession shop in the hotel before leaving.

To Millie the beach was like heaven. All she could do was focus on the water and the beach. The water was warm, and the sand was a grainy tan with the sun beaming down. The girls talked while relaxing on towels and under red and white umbrellas provided at no charge at the grass-roofed beach hut. There was a background of the sight and sound of seagulls and small waves rolling onto the beach.

They ate hotdogs and drank beer for lunch. The food shack accepted German marks without hesitation. The beach was crowded with people. The beach remained crowded most of the day until it closed at 3 p.m. Jane struck up a conversation with an Italian man who spoke German while they all dined on their hotdogs and beer. Closing time came too fast. Before they knew it, the shuttle from the hotel was waiting for them in the beach parking lot. Once the people left, so did the seagulls. Millie, having had her fill of sand, sea, and sun, dozed off on the return trip to the hotel.

Upon their return to the hotel, Jane was stopped by the concierge and told there was a message waiting for her at the front desk. Jane picked up a small, folded manila-colored card and they all returned to their respective rooms. In their room, Millie noticed Jane's reaction to the message.

Jane said quietly, "Oh rats!" She threw the card into her pocketbook.

Millie nervously laughed at her comment. She wondered if it had anything to do with what Frieda told her.

"Never mind, it's only about work."

But Millie was surprised by the reaction.

After that, no other comments were made about the message as they dressed for a casual dinner at the small restaurant, "Little Mineta" next door to the hotel. The girls' dinner involved lively talking about their beach experience, particularly about the handsome Italian men. They all had traditional spaghetti and meatballs, with a delicious side salad, and a glass of local red wine to christen their meal in Italy. Getting to sleep that night even with a slight sunburn was easy. It was all good.

The next day could have been a carbon copy of the day before. Jane even got into a conversation with the same good-looking Italian man from yesterday. He brought along three friends this time. Unfortunately, the three friends did not speak any German, only Italian, but were friendly and spent most of the day in the water with the girls.

The next day, Jane checked out of the rooms at 7 a.m., and they were back on the road to Germany. As they left the hotel, they heard from the concierge who spoke fluent German, that since Germany had invaded Austria, thousands more prisoners were being sent to Dachau as well as other prison camps. This greatly influenced the chatter in the car on the return trip. The girls talked of how even more prisoners would increase the number of SS guards to feed. In their minds they were already returning to camp without being there. It made for a stressed ride home. It was not good.

7

MR. STEIN

Several months passed after the trip to Genoa. It was back to the grind every day. One day, early in the afternoon, there was a problem with a drain on the large three compartment sink used for washing pots and pans in the kitchen. Millie's familiarity with construction told her that poor drainage of a sink was usually a blockage somewhere in the sewer pipe system. In a conference with Frieda, Renee, and Millie, they all decided that they needed help from a plumber. Frieda called Jane and asked for a prisoner skilled as a plumber to come to help.

The prisoners, some of whom were experienced in the building trades, performed odd jobs around the camp. Jane said she would find a plumber and send him over. Late in the afternoon, a man was escorted by a guard through the high wire double fence gate to the staff kitchen.

The man was old and could not work in the field anymore. He had been at the prison camp for about three months and worked odd plumbing jobs in the prisoner barracks. Most prisoners were used as slave labor to manufacture weapons and other war materials for Germany.

Number 140523 as he was known was a certified plumber before he and his family were rounded up outside Krakow with other Jews and sent on an overcrowded train to Dachau. Upon his arrival at Dachau after traveling for days in a wooden box car with many others, as he and his family exited the train car, he was selected to help with construction of new structures which would eventually become the ovens that would incinerate many prisoners. His wife and children were sent to the barracks with many others while he was sent to the barracks for construction workers. He never saw his family again. For about a month he was a commando, a prisoner who helped the guards with other prisoners and work crews. His knowledge of plumbing was very good, so he was used frequently during construction and repair at the camp. He arrived at the kitchen in a dirty striped uniform with a six pointed star patch on it. He was very thin and frail. He smelled like urine and feces. He looked tired, overworked, and underfed. Millie was asked by the guard to take them both to the backed-up sink. The man walked very slowly behind Millie. Millie was feeling sick to her stomach thinking that his family was killed, and he was forced into slave labor as a plumber for the Nazis because they were Jews.

After several minutes, the man disconnected the sink trap with tools he had brought in a cloth tool bag, cleaned out the blockage which was small piece of rag and pieces of food, reconnected the trap and tested the water flow. Everything was now in order. The man touched Millie's hand, with his dirty hands, as he put his tools into the cloth bag. He looked up at her with tear-filled eyes. Millie gave him a clean towel to wipe the dirt from his hands.

As the guard was talking with Frieda to the side, the man said to Millie in a low trembling almost indistinguishable voice, "You know what to do." Did he mean after watching him work that she could clear the pipes herself or did he mean that something would come into her life and she would inherently know what to do? Millie became aware that something sinister was going on.

The guard finished conversing with Frieda and grabbed the man by the right arm as he carried his tool bag in the other and escorted him out of the building. They walked slowly through the gate into the fenced yard and disappeared into one of the barracks.

Millie's heart was beating hard and strong. She felt her body start to sweat and tingle all over. What was she supposed to do, she wondered?

She returned to her work cleaning tables. She desperately wanted to talk to someone. She thought of Jane since, perhaps, she could find out what was going on from her perspective working in administration.

Prisoners like the man, Mr. Stein, were war criminals.

What did she know?

8

JANE'S HOUSE

It would be several long days before Millie thought through the traumatic event with Mr. Stein, until she got up the nerve to talk to her friend Jane. It was after work on a Friday as she was headed to dinner in the staff dining building and Jane was in her car, headed to her house. It was a brief encounter.

"Hey, Jane."

"Hi there, Millie."

"Where can we talk privately?"

"Come with me to my house? Okay? I'll wait in the parking lot for you to change. Hey, you can eat with us."

"Swell, Jane. Give me ten minutes."

"See you then."

After changing and letting Frieda know where she was going, Millie got into Jane's car, and they headed out of the camp to John and Jane's house nearby.

Jane turned off the paved road, at a yellow mailbox, through a break in the woods into her driveway. John and Jane's home was a small, colorful, and pretty country-style wood frame house with a separate garage that had a crushed stone driveway. It was only seven miles from the camp. It had a small front porch with a canopy. On one of the wooden porch columns they flew the Nazi flag. The house was nestled in the woods on a small cleared grassed plot. Because of the way the house was sited, it was not visible from the paved road. Jane pulled up to the garage. She got out, opened the garage door, and then pulled slowly into her garage. Jane closed the garage door and she and Millie walked together from the garage on a short brick path up to the front door of the house. Jane unlocked the door. As Jane turned on the lights, they entered into a beautifully decorated living room. John was not home. He was working the late shift at the motor pool.

"I knew you would want to talk about Mr. Stein. I am glad you came to me." Jane said as she looked Millie in the eyes. "What took you so long?"

Millie gazed at Jane and said, "What is going on at the camp?"

Jane asked Millie to sit down at the dining room table and bought her a glass of water. She brought one for herself too.

"I can imagine your shock being approached by Mr. Stein: Shocked at his awful condition, his dirty uniform with its six-pointed fabric star. However, he is one of the valuable prisoners because of his plumbing expertise. He does a lot of repair and maintenance work around the camp. He is an expert at his trade and can be trusted. However, I need to tell you that your feelings about Germany may be misplaced. When the camp first opened, most prisoners were political or war criminals. Now the camp is also being flooded with Jews. The camp is overcrowded and the prisoners are not properly or humanely taken care of. They are used as slaves at the camp and on projects outside the camp. They are worked to death."

Millie replied, "When I left America, with all of its problems, I thought Germany was going to be perfect. I am quite shocked. I came all this way to get away from problems. Our life at the camp and our friendship has been so much fun. Now this."

Jane commented, "Hitler is becoming more powerful every day, but he has what is referred to as a Jewish problem. As he is conquering countries in Europe, more and more Jews are being taken as prisoners. Hitler hates the Jews."

"What are you saying, Jane? That Germany is against Jews? Is that what Mr. Stein was trying to tell me?"

"Yes, Millie. I also have something to tell you."

"Okay, Jane. What other bubble are you going to burst for me?"

Jane paused.

"Please understand I am your friend and I trust you. I hope you will help us, like Mr. Stein asked. John and I are part of the Resistance movement. We are fighting to free Germany from Hitler and his Nazi henchmen that are taking over all of Europe with an evil totalitarian government."

All Millie could do was stare at Jane while she spoke. When Jane stopped talking, Millie began to cry. Jane, whether she wanted to or not, did burst Millie's bubble. Millie's nerves were on edge. She was even bothered by the ticking of the cuckoo clock on the wall. She did not know how to respond to Jane, a person she really liked and trusted. She took a drink of water. She excused herself, got up from her chair, and went outside to the porch off the dining room to think. Where would she place her trust? Would it be with Hitler or her friend Jane?

After several minutes, Millie thought through the situation she was in. She remembered her father telling her to carefully consider your next move in a game of chess. She carefully considered what she was to say to Jane. She then came back inside and dried her eyes. Inside the house, Jane was making some coffee, ham sandwiches, and cutting up a homemade cinnamon and pecan coffee cake. The sun was a couple of minutes from completely setting. Long shadows were cast on the little house.

Millie sat at her place at the dining room table.

When Jane finished setting the table and bringing in the food, Millie said, "Jane, I have always trusted you. I have always been loyal. You have always been helpful to me without any drama. We have had fun together. If I am to join you then I have to know the risks and rewards of joining the Resistance. I came a long way to join the Third Reich and need to know more…before I become…a traitor."

"That's fair enough. What do you need to know? Know that we are highly confidential, even above top secret in some cases. However, I may be able answer some questions."

"How many of you are there? Where do you meet? Who else that we know is involved? What is our fate if exposed? What am I obligated to do?"

Jane cleared her throat, looked away, and batted her eye lashes quickly several times, knew she was putting herself at extreme risk by answering these pointed questions, and quietly said, "I do not know how many there are, we do not meet as a group, the leaders are high-level government officials or German leaders, several people we know are involved, and you may have some assignments. That's all I can tell you now, but if you are willing to join us, let me know. I will be your control."

"Where and when, Jane?"

"I will let you know. Do not breathe a word of what we have discussed to anyone. Just you coming to my house may be viewed with suspicion."

Feeling somewhat trapped, but also knowing what she had observed at the camp and the added intrigue of Mr. Stein, Millie agreed.

The girls had their dinner of excellent coffee, ham sandwiches, and coffee cake.

Jane told her if she was approached with the comment, "Did Jane talk to you?" It must be responded to with the comment, "Of course, my friend."

In the pitch darkness, not a word was said as Jane drove Millie back to the camp.

9

A GRAND MISSION

After Kristallnacht in November of 1938, severe measures were taken against Jews in Germany. On November 9, 1938, synagogues were burned, and Jewish schools and businesses were attacked, burned, and looted. Trains were arriving every day at the prison camp loaded with men, women, and children, Jews taken not as prisoners of war but only because they were Jewish. Prejudice and hatred were alive in Nazi Germany.

Because of the growing war effort in Germany, Millie and several other girls including Marsha were assigned to the Eagles Nest. The kitchen there was smaller than the kitchen at the Dachau camp. The kitchen was first class, since Hitler and his staff were there on a regular basis. Millie and Marsha had been at the Eagles Nest for only four months when, on a Friday, Herman Goering and several of this staff arrived for a secret meeting over the weekend.

The kitchen staff was put on high alert. Food, wine, and beer were delivered and stored or refrigerated as needed. The dining area was thoroughly cleaned and disinfected.

Light bulbs were changed and the outside was swept clear of leaves and dirt. The place looked great. It was a concrete block building with large interior rooms for official meetings and entertaining. Weddings were held there as well as parties for the officials of the government. This was the first time that Goering had visited since Millie and Marsha had started working at the Eagles Nest. Goering's staff consisted of about a dozen military officers, his secretary, and his valet. Millie and Marsha inspected each other to make sure they were looking good. They were. Millie would be meeting with her contact.

It was after a fine dinner of prime rib, fried red potatoes, green beans, coffee, tea, and sparkling water, with apple pie for dessert. After all was cleaned up, refreshments were brought in. All charts and maps on the walls and tables were covered by black tarps for security purposes. After the refreshments were set on a large side table, and the big solid wood doors to the conference room were locked from the inside, Goering's meeting began. It went well into the night.

Millie, Marsha, and the rest of the staff waited in the kitchen to be able to provide more food and drink for the long meeting. About midnight, some of the kitchen staff retreated to their rooms to go to bed. Then Millie and Marsha heard the meeting room door to the kitchen unlock. An SS officer left the meeting room and entered the kitchen to request the kitchen staff prepare more coffee since the coffee in the heated urn in the meeting room was running low. Immediately, two kitchen staff went to get the empty urn. The SS Officer's name was Captain Alfred Berger. He was assigned to Dachau as one of the training staff for new SS recruits. At the time, Dachau was being used as a training camp for SS Prison Guards. Captain Berger asked Millie to make some more coffee. She said she would.

He then asked, "Did Jane talk with you?"

To which Millie said, "Of course, my friend."

"Then in that case, I have something for you."

Captain Berger reached into his jacket pocket, took out a small paper tube and gave it to Millie. He then quickly returned to the meeting. After setting up a new pot of coffee, Millie wheeled it into the meeting room with its covered top secret walls and then went to the ladies restroom. She sat on the last water closet and closed the stall door. The passing of the tube and Millie's trip to the restroom went unnoticed by everyone including the weary kitchen crew. The light from the candelabra reflecting off of the dark wood ceiling in the restroom gave enough light for Millie to read the hand written note rolled up inside the cardboard tube. The note read:

Remove Enigma machine from office.
Bring to Hotel zum Turken.
Room 112.

This is what Jane told her would happen. And it was happening. She was not afraid. She did not wait, but walked to the office which was next to the meeting room. She had seen an enigma machine once at the prison camp on Jane's desk. So she knew what to look for. The one she was looking for in the office was about 11 inches by 13.5

inches by 6 inches and weighed about 26 pounds. It was the M3 version. It was the Wehrmacht Enigma used by the German Air Force.

The small office off the main corridor was not locked or occupied but the lights were on. She could hear the sound of the fan set up in the office. She could hear the loud voices and talking through the wall from the meeting in the adjacent room. She quickly looked around for the enigma machine in its wood box. It was on the floor next to the wood desk. She removed the wood box with its prized contents from the office, quietly closed the office door, and brought the box unnoticed down the dimly lit corridor to her bedroom below. This mission had just started.

Millie, her heart beating wildly, did not return to the kitchen. She stashed the wood box in her locker and draped a towel over it. She undressed, took a fast shower, and went directly to bed. Soon other Eagles Nest staff were returning to the living quarters.

Marsha asked, "Millie, are you feeling okay?"

"Yes, okay, but really tired tonight."

"Okay. Then I will see you in the morning."

The next day, Goering and his staff left after breakfast. The meeting room had to be cleaned, as well as the kitchen, but the staff had the rest of the day off. Millie asked Marsha if she wanted to go have lunch at the Hotel zum Turken, nearby the Eagles Nest. Marsha thought it was a great idea since they always liked a change, to be served rather than to be serving others. They left the building taking the elevator to the ground floor where there were several taxis waiting.

Marsha did not ask Millie about the extra luggage, in this case a wood box, as they got into the taxi.

"Hotel zum Turken, please," said Millie.

The two girls settled in for the short ride to the hotel. The day was warm and sunny as the taxi weaved its lonely way on the country roads toward the hotel. The girls opened the rear windows of the car. The fresh air was welcome to them blowing their hair around. The mountain region around Berchtesgaden was beautiful and exhilarating. They both enjoyed the ride.

Millie and Marsha split the fare. They arrived at the hotel as some conference was being held but were able to get a table in the crowded dining room. The room had a high ceiling with many dark wood beams, several ornate chandeliers, and paintings of local interest on the walls. The tables and chairs were ornately carved heavy dark wood. The front desk tagged their bags and placed them in a small private closet off the main staircase. Millie thought this was most convenient. Then the girls went to their table in the dining room and ordered lunch.

For lunch, they both ordered ham and cheese sandwiches with German potato salad on the side and chocolate ice cream for dessert. After ordering, Millie excused herself and headed for the restroom off the lobby. She was familiar with its location next to the stairway on the way to the restaurant. Millie walked to the closet, while motioning to the front desk concierge on the way. He nodded. Millie took the wood box from the closet and headed from the lobby to the main hallway looking for room 112. She knocked on the door. But no answer. She knocked again. She waited about ten seconds. Before she was about to knock again, a man in a dark blue robe and leather slippers opened the door slightly and extended his hand. He was a short overweight man. He was about thirty years old with a small mustache and thinning hair. He was wearing black framed reading glasses. He asked her if she had spoken to Jane.

To which Millie replied, "Of course, my friend."

She then handed him the wooden box. As he grabbed the box handle, he pulled the valuable box inside the room and quickly closed the door. Millie felt a rush and awe that she was involved in some small way in the Resistance. Then she quickly returned to Marsha in the loud smoke-filled crowded restaurant.

The continuous talking and clinking glasses and plates with a little smoke, created an exciting environment. Marsha remarked that while she was waiting she noticed two men she thought were good looking having drinks at a table nearby. Both wore fancy dark suits and ties. Millie looked over at the two men and agreed with Marsha. After a couple of minutes, the girl's lunch arrived.

As they dined, Millie noticed the man in the robe, this time in a dark suit and tie, carrying the wooden box and another suitcase, breezing by the opening to the restaurant from the lobby heading for the front doors. As he disappeared outside, the two men in suits and ties in the restaurant quickly got up and followed him outside to a waiting vehicle. Millie and Marsha just smiled at each other as the two men left the restaurant. Millie knew the three men were part of the Resistance. So did Marsha.

To the girls' surprise, a piano started playing to accompany their lunch.

10

RETURN TO DACHAU

It seemed to Millie that after serving at the Eagles Nest for several months, both Marsha and her services were no longer needed. With very little to do, on Monday of the following week, another beautiful day in southern Germany, both Millie and Marsha received orders to transfer back to Dachau. They expected reassignment.

They packed up their gear, took the elevator to the ground floor, and boarded a small military bus which regularly stopped outside the entrance to the tunnel and elevator at Eagles Nest. This bus was scheduled every hour on the hour daily for a ride to and from the Eagles Nest and Dachau. The ride was relatively short but there were several stops along the way. At the last stop, there was no more room on the small bus, so several enlisted men had to wait for the next bus.

When the girls arrived at Dachau camp, it was still a warm sunny day. However, the camp was very crowded with prisoners and also guards. A train loaded with men, women, and children was arriving at the unloading platform inside the camp's fenced area as their bus entered the camp. The atmosphere and activity they were watching inside the fenced area was grim and caused both Marsha and Millie to gasp in horror.

After being gone for several months, the camp had changed. From where they could see at the bus stop, the new arrivals disembarking the train were being segregated into groups. From there, some were selected out of the groups to perform special activities. Others were selected to be commandos. Commandos were selected as team leaders working directly for the guards. They helped the guards in managing the prisoners. All able workers, men and women, were selected to work as slaves. Others not able to work, including the elderly and children, were sent to the gas chambers to be killed and eventually to the ovens to be incinerated. Due to the constant influx of people and overcrowding, it was planned that all prisoners were eventually to be killed. This was the final solution for Hitler's hatred of the Jews.

After witnessing the horrible things going on at the camp, Marsha and Millie slowly retreated into their barracks. They quickly unpacked, took a shower, and then made their bunks with clean sheets and pillowcases from the storage room at the back of the barracks building. The barracks were empty except for a kitchen worker who was sick and asleep in her bunk at the end of the barracks near the storage room. Many of the windows were open on such a nice afternoon which made the girls feel at home. They showered and put on their uniforms from their locker. Both girls were headed to the kitchen.

Marsha said, "Good luck, sweetie."

Millie said, "We will need all the luck we can get."

As they left the barracks, Millie saw Lyman and several other officers going into the dining hall. Dinner would be served shortly so the girls hustled to get to the kitchen as quickly as they could. As they walked up the three concrete steps to the back entrance to the kitchen, Frieda Miller greeted them. She welcomed them back each with a hug. She told them there were many changes to the camp. She could see they were upset and told them not to be disturbed, but to continue their jobs as before. Strangely, she did not look them in the eye. The girls looked for the list of assignments for the day on the cork-board next to the back door. According to the schedule that day, Frieda assigned them to clean up tables and wash dishes. Throughout dinner, the dining area was unusually very loud and overcrowded.

After several hours, one large table was still occupied. This table with Lyman and other officers was very loud. As Millie passed by the table, Lyman reached out and gently touched her elbow.

"Millie, can we have another round of coffee? In fact, bring a whole new pot for us."

"Very well, Lyman."

He said, "Has Jane talked to you?"

Millie walked away, her eyes fixated on Lyman, she said to him, "Of course, my friend."

Then he too was in the Resistance. So, there were military types as well as civilian types in the Resistance.

The percolator coffee pot was ready in about 10 minutes. Millie remembered to add a tablespoon of salt to the coffee grounds before brewing. The coffee pot was loaded onto a small steel gurney and wheeled over to Lyman's table. There were about a dozen officers at the table. Through an open window, Millie could see a large crowd of prisoners in their dirty striped uniforms up against the fence surrounding the nearest prison barracks. Faces of many prisoners were meanly smashed into the wire fence. Guards were shouting. Prisoners were screaming. Prisoners who fell and could not get up were trampled. Some to their death. Prisoners were being whipped with chains and pounded with wood timbers. Many were injured and bleeding. A cloud of dust was quickly rising over the near end of the camp from these brutal activities in the dirt covered yards between the many barracks.

While this was going on outside, four musicians carrying their instruments, music, and stands entered the dining hall through the back door. They were dressed in formal attire. Millie saw two violins, one cello, and one bass. Frieda greeted them cordially. They set up in the corner near the officer's table. It was a brutal contrast to the mayhem going on outside. After tuning their instruments, they played several works from Eine Kline Nachtmusik by Bach. Each piece was greeted with applause from the seated officers. The musicians were professionals who lived in a separate barracks. They had been performing at the commandant's request for about one month. They were all captured prisoners from Munich who played in the local orchestra. They were Jews. They played for about one hour and left to a standing ovation from the smiling German officers. They left the dining hall and quickly returned to their special barracks away from the chaos in the yard.

That night there were many executions at the far end of the camp. The paved area behind a high concrete wall was lit up with high flood lights. During the executions, other unpaved areas of the camp with barracks were dimly lit. Prisoners were being selected to either be sent to the firing squad or to newly constructed gas chambers. Also, the ovens were being fired up to incinerate as many bodies as possible during the night. Millie saw Lyman and the officers at his table slowly walking outside. They were the firing squad. Millie and the other mess hall help returned to their barracks. Prisoners were returned to their barracks as well. Except for the sound of gunfire at the far end of the camp, all was quiet.

The next morning seemed like any other day. But it would not be.

The next day would be November 9, 1938. It was the beginning of the Kristallnacht pogrom which would last for three long days. While the propaganda against Jews and persecution of Jews had been going on for a while, the Nazis at the highest level of the organization planned Kristallnacht to kill Jews, destroy their synagogues and businesses, and confiscate their homes and items of value. About 100 Jews were killed and over 1000 synagogues were burned. After invading Czechoslovakia and Austria, large numbers of Jews emigrated out of Germany, Czechoslovakia, and

Austria. Many unfortunate Jews who could not emigrate ended up in concentration camps like Dachau. The population of prisoners at Dachau increased beyond capacity. The firing squads, gas chambers, and ovens were overworked. A guillotine was used for severely radical prisoners.

Prisoners were essentially slaves and were systematically being worked to death. The prisoners were mostly German people who had been classified out of German society. The diabolical scheme was to remove undesirables from German society to form a perfect Aryan race. This utopian oriented race theory being implemented by the German political leaders was anything but perfect. The people in German prison camps were being held against their will as if they were convicted of a crime. In fact, the so-called perfect race was committing horrible crimes. There was no way out of the concentration camps for prisoners except death.

Millie was so happy to join the Nazi movement when she arrived in Germany many years ago. However, the Nazis had turned from an organization for the people of Germany into an organization against the people of Germany and also other countries in Europe. Things had gotten out of control. She used to hear people say, "If Hitler only knew about these horrible things going on he would stop them." In fact, Hitler was behind all the horrible things being carried out in the name of creating a perfect race.

Millie was now convinced that Hitler was a godless dictator, not a benevolent man of the people. She was angry at herself for leaving her family, traveling far from home, and joining the Nazi movement. It was wrong.

In fact, Millie was now firmly, more than ever, committed to the Resistance.

PUNISHMENT AND REWARD

Millie and Marsha worked at Dachau without much fanfare for about three years after their return from The Eagles Nest. On a particularly cold Friday in March, 1941, both of them were asked to meet with the camp Director in his office. Millie recalled the office from her first day at Dachau. It's where she was introduced to Jane by Lyman. She had not been there since. She remembered the office to be well decorated, as it was when she and Marsha entered. Jane nodded but did not speak to them as they passed her desk. There were three officers, all of them Gestapo, and the current Camp Director, Colonel Schmitz, in attendance. The Camp Director asked them to sit at the opposite end of the rectangular glass topped mahogany conference table. The girls were nervous and showed it. Even Col. Schmitz was nervous. The three Gestapo were hunting for criminals.

The Camp Director said, "You are here to answer questions about your time at the Eagles Nest. Do not be nervous or afraid."

JOHN SNELL

He pulled out a sheet of paper with writing on it.

He began with a question, "Millie and Marsha, were you aware that Field Marshal Goering was holding a meeting there while you were on duty?"

Quickly, they both answered, "Yes."

"Do you remember anything being removed from the office near the conference room?"

Both girls both answered, "No."

"Were either of you girls in the office for any reason?"

Again, they both emphatically answered, "No."

One of the Gestapo officers sitting next to Col. Schmitz leaned forward, cleared his throat, adjusted his wire frame glasses and with a smirk asked, "Did either of you take anything from the office there?"

"We both worked in the kitchen and served meals and food for the conference, but it was three years ago. I do not remember much," said Millie without hesitation, looking him straight in the eye.

"That goes for me too," said Marsha.

Both girls realized by the questioning they would have to fight hard not to be accused of something. In her mind, Millie knew what they were after, but did not let on. If she was accused of anything criminal it would not be false. Both girls were lying. At that time, as Marsha finished speaking, Jane opened the door and entered the Director's office to hand him a note. He then excused himself and quickly left his office. One could hear automatic machine gunfire coming from the barracks nearest the administration building. Left with the three Gestapo officers and without their camp Director, the girls began shaking in their seats, like being at a horror movie.

Millie remembered Lyman telling her, "Be the captain of your own ship." This remembrance helped stop the shaking.

The Gestapo officers looked at each other but had nothing to say except, "Thank you, ladies. We will be in touch with Col. Schmitz." Then they rose, gave the Nazi salute, to which the girls responded, and left the office. As Millie and Marsha were left alone looking at each other in the large office, Jane re-entered and complimented the girls on their answers. She said, "Things seem to be coming to a head. Be very wary of who talks to you. And keep the faith." Then Jane turned and escorted the girls back to the kitchen. It was then that Millie found out about Marsha.

"You too?" asked Millie.

"Yup," Marsha responded.

It was a good thing. Both girls felt invigorated.

About a month passed after the infamous meeting with the Gestapo. The camp became so overcrowded with prisoners that new guards were trained and added. Also, the dining hall for guards was now open 24 hours a day for full meals. The kitchen staff was split into three shifts, at eight hours each. New girls were added too. Things were definitely getting out of hand. Millie and Marsha expected the worst.

Then, one early morning in the dark, Millie was woken from her sleep by two Gestapo guards. They told her to put on a dress they were holding made out of a burlap material. She removed her sleeping nightgown and put on the dress by the light of a flashlight held by one of the guards. The whole thing looked very bad at this point. With the guard's flashlight they all left the building without turning on the lights or waking anyone else. Frieda did not appear to wake up. They all got into a small black van with a large swastika on the side, guards in front, Millie in the back, which was waiting outside the back entrance to the women's barracks building. As Millie looked at the building as they were driving away, she thought it was for the last time. She was right. As she was dressing in the burlap dress given to her, she managed to get a hold of her locker key, which she held tightly in her left hand.

The truck cleared by prison guards entered the gates on the prisoner side of the camp. It was the middle of the night. Lights were on inside some of the barracks as torture for the prisoners. Several barracks had prisoners marching around them in the dark as punishment. There were prisoners lined up to be shot by a firing squad down at the end of the far driveway.

Millie started to cry as the truck rumbled along towards the far end of the prisoner area to a small black concrete block building. The relatively new structure was about 15 feet wide and maybe 50 feet long and unusually high. She had not seen this building before. It was well hidden from the rest of the camp. It was surrounded by a high reinforced metal fence and by a small forest of pine trees. The truck proceeded through a gate in the fence manned by a pair of Gestapo guards and was parked at the rear entrance to the building. The building was operated by the Gestapo separate from the camp. A commando in his dirty striped uniform escorted Millie through a large steel door to a small waiting room at the rear of the building. There were several other prisoners, one man and two women, already under guard in the waiting room. They were not Jews. They were affiliated with the "White Rose" student resistance organization. They each wore a burlap dress, both men and women. They knew they were to be killed. They did not know how.

The small waiting room which smelled like extreme body odor was painted black with an exposed concrete floor. It contained a long unpainted wooden bench along the side wall and was lit only by a single light bulb hanging from the high concrete ceiling maybe fifteen feet above them. A large steel door, like the one they entered through into the waiting room, at the far end of the room opened into the "death-room." This "death-room" had a red quarry tile floor, with several floor drains and a six-foot-high white tile wainscot. Above the wainscot the walls were painted black. The ceiling was very high. Maybe fifteen feet or so. In addition to the guillotine and its accessories, the "death-room" contained a water hose, a large table and sink, and at the far end a movie camera and a still camera. As the door was opened the prisoners could see inside because in contrast to the waiting room it was very brightly lit. The lighting was so bright it was blinding.

The first prisoner escorted into the "death room" was the young man, in his early twenties. His crime was embezzlement. He committed no crime. He was arrested yesterday. Crimes were made up, not based in reality. There was no trial. He was to be killed for being a member of the Resistance. He was walked to the bench in front of the guillotine by two commandos and was made to lie down on his stomach. As he struggled to put his head in the cage beneath the shining blade it was quickly cut off.

The movie camera filmed the entire operation. The still camera took photos.

After some minimal clean-up of the room the next prisoner was killed. And the next until it was Millie's turn. Both of the women prisoners were raped before they were beheaded, so Millie prepared mentally for her fate. As the door to the "death-room" swung open she noticed a change in the appearance of the room. This time the lighting was not so bright. A tall man in a camp guard uniform was standing in and blocking the doorway. He was holding a Mauser rifle and had a Luger pistol in a holster on his belt, both with silencers. As Millie stood up, he shot the Gestapo guards, the commandos, the movie camera operator, and the still camera man. At the same time, because her anger had built up as she faced certain death, even though she was not a violent person, Millie stabbed the remaining commando in the neck with the locker key. As the wounded commando was flinching from her attack, the man with the Mauser also shot him dead. The man with the Mauser and Millie were the only people left alive in the building of death.

The man then shouted, "I'm Col. West and I'm here to save you!"

Millie who was terrified and had been caught off guard by a change in the proceedings shouted back after several seconds of delay, "It's about time, big guy!" They quickly ran out of the building. Millie was crying.

"Thank you, sir. Thank you." She screamed.

Waiting outside in the dark behind the building was the empty parked van. Its former driver and a guard were lying motionless on the ground each with a bullet from the Mauser in their heads. Both were shot dead. Col. West told Millie to jump into the back of the van and cover herself with a tarp that he brought for the escape. At this time in the early morning there was no one around. He drove the van slowly to not attract attention, along the road next to the barracks, to the main gate of the camp. Wearing his camp uniform and with Millie hidden in the back of the van, Col. West, in what appeared to be an empty van, was easily cleared though the main gate and followed a curving paved road through the woods to the Hotel zum Turken. The mission was a success, so far.

After several hours they arrived at the Hotel zum Turken. The owner, Karl Schuster, was rather outspoken in his disapproval of the Nazis. Locals were being encouraged to sell their properties to the Nazis. Shuster refused to sell. He got into trouble after Hitler established his home in the house next door. He was tortured at Dachau until he agreed to sell. After the sale he was allowed to live and manage the hotel for the Third Reich. He threatened to divulge the horror of the Third Reich but was allowed to live.

Col. West slowly entered the circular driveway at the back of the hotel. He could make out only two uniformed guards at the entrance to the hotel grounds. It was very dark without outside lights. The guards left them alone. The truck slowly crept to a stop at the loading dock which was just outside the kitchen. Col. West told Millie not to move and stay hidden under the tarp. They waited at the dock about ten minutes until two uniformed men exited the dark building onto the dock. They were Karl Shuster and General Frederick Olbricht, a leader of the German Army Resistance.

"You will receive your orders here from General Olbricht, who I am assisting. He is one of the leaders of the Resistance group," said Col. West.

"Okay, but who the hell are you?" a frustrated Millie answered.

"Briefly, I am the son of your father's friend, statesman Roy Owen West from Chicago. I am with the American Office of Secret Service, the OSS," he responded calmly.

"What is your first name?"

"Call me Charlie. Normally, we do not use names."

Millie brushed off some pine needles from her burlap dress as she said, "Okay, Charlie. Great job on rescuing me!"

Gen. Olbricht in German Army Uniform exited the dark building and came down the concrete stair from the loading dock carrying a flashlight and a small valise with a military uniform inside for Millie. It was a complete female uniform for the German Army, with the rank of sergeant, including hat, stockings, and shoes. An Army Colonel,

Claus von Stauffenberg, a member of the Resistance, who would later be involved in a failed attempt to kill Hitler, was barely visible standing in the doorway off the loading dock with Mr. Shuster, keeping a lookout for the General. The General looked around the yard as he invited Millie to come inside and change clothes while Colonel West waited quietly in the truck. Inside the building, Millie took a quick shower and changed clothes lit only by a flashlight given to her by Colonel von Staffenberg. After she changed clothes, and before giving her instructions, the General asked her if she could remember some short instructions.

Millie said, "Well…yes, sir, General Olbricht."

The General said, "Millie, you are a very brave woman. That is why you have been promoted to sergeant. Just so you know, the Enigma Machine you stole for us from the Eagles Nest was transported via aircraft and safely arrived in England. We rescued you from Dachau in response to a high-level request from one of our covert contacts with the American government to return you to America. What is happening now is part of the plan. Be careful and be safe please. Do not trust anyone outside the Resistance. In case anyone asks, you will be Sergeant Bauer and you will work for me."

Mille responded, "Thank you, General. I am proud to be a member of your Resistance."

And that was that.

The General's verbal orders were for her to get a room at the hotel and wait until morning. Check in as Sergeant Bauer and then wait there for a visitor. Millie and Charlie drove around to the hotel front parking lot and waited there in the truck until after the hotel opened for business. The hotel guards, probably working for the Resistance, ignored them. They booked a room and waited. Charlie told her that his mission was to get her, and others, out of Germany and back to America. They cleaned themselves up as best they could.

"Failure is not an option," he said as he put his hand on her shoulder and looked at her with a slight smile. She gave Charlie a much-needed hug and cried on his shoulder. It did not take much for them to fall asleep that night. They slept in separate beds.

12

THE MYSTERIOUS MISSION

The weather on that day in 1941 was sunny but rather chilly with light snow during the night. Germany was invading Russia so many soldiers were at the Eastern Front. The Resistance was growing in power to combat the Nazis. The war with Russia on the eastern front was not going in Germany's favor. It was referred to as the "war of annihilation." The Germans were getting beat up badly by the Russians.

There were four German guards that were stationed at the Hotel zum Turken, mostly for show, although they were armed. Millie and Charlie looked out the window which faced the front entrance and parking lot, waiting for a contact. At about eleven o'clock, a large black Nazi van, larger than the one they drove in on, rather slowly pulled up to the hotel's front entrance. Two armed men in German Army uniforms, who were assigned to the Berghof nearby walked into the hotel entrance and disappeared from view. Millie hoped that these men were their contact and were headed to their room. However, they could be out to get them instead. They both looked around to see that they had not left anything behind and then checked out each other's uniforms.

In a few minutes, they heard a knock on the door. Charlie opened the door but kept the security latch on. Through the small opening they saw two German Army Sergeants.

One of them said, "Sergeant Bauer."

In response, Charlie said, "Yes. Come in."

Charlie undid the security latch, opened the door, and the two uniformed armed men entered the room. Charlie looked both ways down the corridor before closing the door.

He then said, "You guys sure are up early."

One of the two men said, "Yeah, wise guy."

The other man said, "You need a ride?"

Millie looked at all three of them and said, "OSS?"

Charlie said, "Yeah. Meet Chris and Henry. Who did you expect?"

The three men laughed together.

Millie then said, "Birds of a feather."

Charlie then said, "This is Millie."

"Hello, Millie," they both said.

After this short introduction, they all went out of the hotel together and into the van waiting out front with its motor running. As Charlie opened the rear door, Millie saw Jane, Marsha, and ten others, including Jane's husband, dressed in military uniform, looking back at her. No words were spoken. In a moment of joy, Millie climbed into the van, hugged Jane and Marsha, sitting on the left side, and then sat down on an open spot on the wooden bench along the right side of the van. Charlie got into the front seat with Chris and Henry. Immediately the van started moving away from the hotel onto the paved road toward a farm several miles north of the center of Obersalzberg.

When the van arrived at the small inconspicuous farm, the passengers were heartily greeted by the farmer Johan and his wife Brittany. They were older people with their children already grown and moved off the farm. They were the von Tresckows. They had Johan's brother Hans staying with them, a member of the civilian resistance and also a worker on the farm. The von Tresckow family was part of the Resistance. The farm had a large bunkhouse which had been used several times to smuggle people out of the country. Johan was a leader of the Resistance in the Obersalzberg area. He and Hans were brothers of the famous Henning von Tresckow in the German Army Resistance. Chris drove the van around back of the farmhouse to the old bunk-house in which Hans was living. The passengers got out of the van and walked in the dark quickly into the bunkhouse building. Chris parked the van around back on a gravel parking spot. Hans, Chris, and Henry covered the van with a large gray tarp held down with heavy concrete blocks on all four corners.

The group of fifteen stayed in the bunkhouse and were well-fed for three days before Mr. Johan von Tresckow gave them a message to be ready to go that evening. He had been in contact with the Resistance on his radio in the farm house. The plan was to have an airplane pick them up and fly them to England. Charlie's contact with other OSS members, via the farm house radio, established a time to meet the aircraft in a fallow field on the farm north of the bunkhouse. Pick up time was 0300 hours military time or three o'clock in the morning: 0 dark thirty. The plan was to wait inside the tree line bordering the field on the east side of the fallow field near the bunk house. Once the plane landed, they would run into the field in the dark and get on the plane. The group bedded down but barely fell asleep.

13

FLIGHT TO FREEDOM

At two o'clock in the morning, farmer Johan woke up the group in the bunkhouse. Some had only slept a few hours. Some not at all. Shortly after awakening, Charlie walked the group to the tree line about one hundred yards from the bunkhouse. A barn cat followed them. There was no moon that evening, a primary reason for making the flight to freedom that night. Only Charlie had a flashlight. It had a red lens. The weather forecast was for mild temperatures and medium clouds during the day. In the morning, there was a light fog over the fallow field. There was no wind. The conditions were perfect.

About a half an hour after assembling at the edge of the adjacent forest, they heard the sound of an airplane approaching from the west. It was an unmarked, black Ford Trimotor flying just above the treetops. Millie and the group watched it slowly bank left, enter the airspace over the field, and gingerly touch down. Then it taxied to about fifty feet from their position using the red flashlight for guidance. The group saw a small ladder at the rear entry door be attached to aircraft from the inside. There were no lights either inside or outside the aircraft. Charlie, Millie, and the brave Resistance group ran as fast as they could to the rear door and its welcoming ladder. Soon after the group boarded the plane, it taxied to the larger area of the fallow field. When the aircraft left the ground, the passengers gave loud applause and cheered. They were airborne away from the Nazis and headed toward England in the west. Charlie, who had been on several rescue operations for the OSS, looked around to see almost everyone on board crying.

You're welcome, Charlie said to himself.

The flight was a long one. Time went by slowly, especially since everyone wanted so much to get out of Germany. The plane never got above twenty-five hundred feet to avoid being picked up by German radar. Because of the distance between the Berchtesgaden area location of the farm and the private landing strip in Bletchley Park, the black renegade unmarked plane had to stop to refuel.

Charlie had arranged through his secure OSS contact to refuel at a private dirt landing strip near Hurth outside Cologne. It was on partially rolling countryside property owned by a famous leader of the Resistance, Carl Friedrich Goerdeler. He was involved in a failed plot to kill Hitler. However, the property was thought to be safe.

They arrived as the sun was setting. It was a gorgeous sunset with thin clouds in the west. As the plane touched down, the passengers all clapped and cheered. A large tanker semi-truck met them at the end of the field. To avoid using flashlights, the ground crew had to move quickly to avoid being detected by anyone. After refueling, the flight crew changed out and brought pork sandwiches and canteens of water for the group. The plane slowly taxied down the field, and turned around to take advantage of the wind direction. Though Charlie did not want to delay any longer for fear of being discovered, he had to wait until it was dark to take off just in case their landing had been seen by anyone sympathetic to the Nazis.

Millie thought about something to say to her friends.

"Never did I think things would turn out like this!" shouted a very tired Millie over the loud sound of the plane's three motors.

"I was hoping!" said an exhausted Jane.

"Me too!" shouted Marsha.

The sound of the three strong motors increased in volume as the airplane took off, barely clearing the tree line, and headed due west.

The second leg of the journey between Hurth and Bletchley Park went smoothly. It was a clear night with light cloud cover slightly illuminated by the waxing moon. The passengers felt like foreigners going to another country. Though they were anticipating arriving, everyone on board fell asleep right after takeoff and remained asleep as the plane roared on over the French countryside. After several hours, the sun rose behind them. A few passengers including Millie, Marsha, and Jane woke up to see small waves in the English Channel glistening below them.

Millie thought what was happening to them was God's plan.

Even so, nowhere was safe until the plane passed over the White Cliffs of Dover. Once again, Millie was struck by their beauty. It had been many years since she witnessed them the first time. This time, they seemed to stand up like a jagged bulwark over the channel and the rest of Europe behind her. She was glad she left Germany.

The metal-sided plane with its valuable passengers banked slightly to line up with the Bletchley Park grass runway. When the plane touched down again, the passengers cried out with laughter and applause. They were safe and in good hands.

Millie thought about what she would tell her parents.

14

BLETCHLEY PARK AND BEYOND

The Ford Trimotor landed safely on the Bletchley Park grass runway. It was the middle of the day. Even though the threat of danger was reduced, England was subjected to bombing runs. The weary passengers were happy to be directed to the headquarters barracks under sunshine in the middle of the day. Since there were a few hours before the debriefing, everyone took a shower, had a decent military meal, and some rest. Their clothes were destroyed. British military fatigue uniforms were provided for them.

Alan Turing, who was primarily responsible for breaking the code on German enigma machines, came into the room where the team was assembled to welcome them to England. He gave special thanks to Jane and Millie for acquiring the Enigma machine that was delivered to him. The Bletchley team used many secrets from that machine to crack the code used for German communications. He stated that knowing the German code will help the Allies defeat the Germans. Then he quickly left the room and wished them all the best. The rest of the meeting was handled by Charlie.

The plan was to leave on a B-17 aircraft the next day and fly to New York City. The group of tired spies was overjoyed and could not wait for tomorrow to arrive. The team meeting adjourned.

The fifteen spies went into the break room to enjoy doing nothing for a change.

They cleaned up and had a great meal in the mess hall.

They spent the night in a large tent, on cots in sleeping bags, like military types.

The next day, the plan changed. Instead of flying home to America, the team with Charlie would take a ship out of Dover. The name of the ship was the Leviathan. Millie remembered the name. The team was shuttled to the port by several small buses so as not to attract attention. They were leaving with the clothes on their back and 100 US dollars in their pocket. When they got to Dover, the ship was docked and boarding a few passengers. Once onboard, the ship left the dock and pointed itself west toward America.

Charlie warned them that the ship may be attacked by German U-boats once in the north Atlantic waters. However, knowing the German communication codes from the stolen Enigma machine helped them locate U-boats. Battleships could then be directed to the location of any threatening U-boats and drop depth charges to destroy them. As the days went on, there were no attacks from submarines or other German ships. It appeared the German Navy was not as strong as it had been. America entering the war had helped the Allies in their war efforts.

On the fifth day after leaving Dover, the ship entered the port of New York City. Millie remembered the docks on the west side of Manhattan. Millie remembered leaving New York those many years ago and her feelings at that time. Had she been a fool? She did not want to think about those old feelings. What happened to her happened. It was a cloudy chilly day, but the sight of New York City warmed Millie's heart as well as the hearts of the other team members. She was thankful to be of service to her country. She was happy to be alive.

As they left the ship down the swaying wooden gangplank, Millie wondered what she would say to the others. Once Jane started her goodbyes, it was not hard for each one to hug each other and wish each other the best. After several minutes, Millie, with tears in her eyes, walked to Grand Central Station with Jane and several others, who were all crying. On their way, the team noticed the traffic, the noise, the tall buildings, and the people. A free people fighting to save the world from the Nazis. Once at the train station, each purchased a ticket to their final destination: Millie to Chicago, Jane and John to Connecticut, and Charlie to Indianapolis. Jane's train left every hour on the hour. Charlie's train left about the same time as Millie's.

Millie still worried about what she would tell her parents and Fred.

Since their trains did not leave for several hours, Millie and Charlie spent time together talking while waiting for their respective trains to depart. Millie realized how thankful she was for Charlie's rescue of her and started to get feelings for him. They had been through some trying times together, but she had not thought about him as anything but her savior from death. He saw her as a prime person in his mission to rescue people from the Nazi threat. He had thought about her as a woman, but pushed those feelings away so he could accomplish his mission. They both thought this was going to be a complicated relationship.

She asked him, "Do you think we could see each other sometime…not right away…but sometime soon?"

Charlie said, "Why, yes, that was going to be my question to you. Can I get your telephone number and address?"

Did I say that properly, thought Charlie?

Millie responded enthusiastically, "Of course, my friend."

Charlie gave her a pencil and paper. She wrote down the precious information and gave the note to a smiling Charlie.

15

HOME AT LAST

After the long train trip, Millie was tired but energized because she was returning home. Her cab ride home, in a Checker Cab from Union Station was uneventful. It was the middle of the day with little traffic. When the cab pulled up to the curb of her parents' house, she had a tingling sensation all over. The house looked the same. The neighborhood was quiet. Across the street, Mr. Buendgen was mowing his beautiful lawn, while smoking his cigar.

Her parents were not expecting her. She knew her mother was home because the fancy lamp in the living room picture window was on. Her father, as well as her brother Fred, was probably working. She could see her mom through the front living room window in her high backed chair reading a book. After all Millie had been through, she did not have trouble knocking on the front door. When her mother opened the door, she immediately hugged Millie and said, "You do not have to say anything. Just you being here is all that counts." Both women stood in the front doorway, hugging each other and crying. It was a long time coming.

They walked through the living room past the ornate lamp and sat down at the dining room table. Her mother asked her if she wanted a cup of coffee. Millie shook her head yes and continued crying. Her mother then said, "Your father will be ecstatic to see you when he gets home. So will Freddy." Her mother headed to the kitchen to get a cup of coffee for Millie.

Millie and her mother talked for several hours. She told her mother everything that was not classified. Then, as a sound came from the living room, as if on cue, Fred walked through the front door. He closed the front door with a smile, ran through the living room, picked up his sister, lifted her off the floor, and spun her around while they both laughed. Their mother placed another cup of hot coffee on the dining room table, after which she clapped, danced, and cheered.

Millie told Freddy that there was not much she could say about the clandestine things in which she participated except to tell them about working in the dining hall at Dachau. Back home it was not well known what the Nazis were doing in their prison camps. As Millie began to fill them in, both her mother and Freddy looked at her in shock and disbelief. After several cups of coffee, her mother called a neighbor to come over to the house: Mr. Hoenig, who worked for the *Chicago Tribune*. Mr. Hoenig would come over tomorrow. Millie took her mother aside to tell her about Charlie. She mentioned only the good parts and nothing secret.

Her mom said, "I am happy that you may have found someone, honey."

The sun was setting through the picture window when Millie's father slowly entered the house through the back door, as was his preference. He was ecstatic to see not only his wife, and son, but his beautiful daughter waiting for him around the dining room table. He dropped his brief-case, slipped off his shoes, and went straight for Millie. He hugged her so hard she was surprised, but she hugged him back just as hard. They both cried.

They remained motionless for a while before her father said, "Don't say anything. Just tell me you are okay."

She shook her head and with tears in her eyes again cried out as she laughed, "I am really okay, really okay, Dad."

"You do not have to tell me anything; just to know you are okay is all I need to know."

Millie did not have to tell her family about any of the details.

Millie was home.

She and Charlie West would marry in Our Savior's Lutheran Church in Chicago, and go on to raise a family in Park Ridge, Illinois. They had one daughter, Ashleigh, and three sons, Chris, John, and Henry. They had two dogs, Max and Jenny. Millie's mom, Julia, lived with them after her father passed away. Julia passed away two months after Millie's father died. Charlie formed a small quality construction company that did well in the post-war economy in Chicago. Later in life, Charlie would sell his company and accept a vice president position with an international construction company based in New York City. After 23 years living in Stamford, Connecticut, living in a large house on a small lake off of High Ridge Road, Charlie would pass away, leaving Millie in the large house, since the kids had moved away and both dogs had died. While living in Connecticut, she and Jane would get together often. They were good friends for many years and enjoyed each other's company until Jane passed away suddenly from an aneurysm. Millie then sold the Connecticut house and moved to an apartment near Central Park in New York City.

You know, the apartment on 72nd near St. James Church.

ACKNOWLEDGMENTS

*Thank you to Lise and Dawn at Windy City Publishers
for their continued expertise in putting this book together.*

*Thank you to my editor Ruth
for making Millie a real hero.*

*Also, thank you to my wife Mary and son Johnny
for their emotional and technical support.*

ABOUT THE AUTHOR

JOHN THOMAS SNELL, SR. was born at Augustana Hospital in Chicago, Illinois on a cold snowy day. He grew up with his mother, father, sister, and Calico the cat in Harwood Heights, just outside Chicago, until he enlisted in the US Army.

Snell graduated from Luther High School North in 1964. He earned a Bachelor of Architecture degree in 1970 from the University of Illinois (Chicago) and a Masters degree in Administrative Science from The Johns Hopkins University in 1983.

Snell served in the army from 1971 to 1974 achieving the rank of Sergeant (Specialist 5). He lived in Louisiana, Missouri, Virginia, and Washington, DC during his years in military service. While in DC, he was a member of the Engineer Strategic Studies Group. After leaving the service with an honorable discharge in 1974 he moved to Columbia, Maryland.

While studying at the University of Illinois, his undergraduate thesis in structural engineering was published jointly with two other colleagues and presented at the Canadian Conference of Applied Mechanics in 1971. Snell went on to become an architect and a professional engineer with active licenses in ten states, and has designed buildings in the USA, Ireland, and Mexico. He has also had several articles on pharmaceutical engineering published in professional journals.

Snell later moved to Connecticut in 1982 and to Florida in 1995. He is currently a practicing architect and professional engineer in Florida. He and his wife Mary live outside of DeFuniak Springs, Florida on lakefront property in an attractive house which he designed. Snell is the proud father of three adult children and grandfather of three sensational grandsons.

Snell is a motorcycle enthusiast and has owned many motorcycles over the years. He is also a model train buff with a fine collection of HO gauge, N gauge, and garden trains.

Snell speaks one language, English, fairly well.

Made in the USA
Columbia, SC
20 July 2023

20669880R00063